"Put Your Arms Around My Neck,"

he murmured and Alyson dreamily complied.

His hands slid over her back to rest on the curve of her hips. "I like the feel of your dress . . . it's like velvet." His sensitive fingers stroked the material. "I'll have to buy you a whole wardrobe of it," he breathed softly. "It's like an extension of your skin. From the first moment I touched you I wanted to discover if the rest of your body has the same texture."

She found herself leaning against him, lost in a helpless excitement such as she'd never experienced before. The warning bells were much too faint to pay any attention to . . .

EDITH ST. GEORGE

is not only an accomplished writer but also a well-known landscape artist. The varied settings of her colorful fiction are as authenic and carefully drawn as her spirited characters.

Dear Reader:

SILHOUETTE DESIRE is an exciting new line of contemporary romances from Silhouette Books. During the past year, many Silhouette readers have written in telling us what other types of stories they'd like to read from Silhouette, and we've kept these comments and suggestions in mind in developing SILHOUETTE DESIRE.

DESIREs feature all of the elements you like to see in a romance, plus a more sensual, provocative story. So if you want to experience all the excitement, passion and joy of falling in love, then SILHOUETTE DESIRE is for you.

Karen Solem
Editor-in-Chief
Silhouette Books

EDITH ST. GEORGE
Velvet Is For Lovers

Silhouette Desire
Published by Silhouette Books New York
America's Publisher of Contemporary Romance

To Bob Huttemeyer,
who was lured by sunken gold
and started this with a small
packet of information.

              With thanks

SILHOUETTE BOOKS, a Division of Simon & Schuster, Inc.
1230 Avenue of the Americas, New York, N.Y. 10020

ISBN: 0-671-49978-5

First Silhouette Books printing September, 1984

10 9 8 7 6 5 4 3 2 1

America's Publisher of Contemporary Romance

Printed in the U.S.A.

BC91

1

But Ecuador! For heaven's sake, why *Ecuador?*" Alyson exploded, her sea-green eyes glinting with exasperation.

"Why not?" Bob returned, his easygoing smile teasing her. "We've never been there before." Which was reason enough for her twin brother, Alyson admitted to herself.

"But you knew I was planning to get our next book ready for the publishers. They've been hounding me ever since they heard we were back." Sometimes Bob's carefree ways drove Alyson crazy. She was proud of the modicum of success the books on their underwater explorations had received, but Bob never seemed to realize the amount of work involved.

"We're not under contract to them," Bob reminded her as he checked the road signs. They'd just left I-95 and were heading to Miami Beach. "Besides, think of all the new pictures that you'll have if I can get you hired for this salvage job."

"I've heard about the Peruvian Current; it sweeps along that coast," she said, aware that she was mentally digging in her heels. "It's still cold from the Antarctic and too turbulent to offer any hope of good pictures."

Alyson shivered at the thought. Their last expedition, off Sicily, had been such a delight with its warm Mediterranean weather. She was momentarily diverted by memories of dark, velvety nights on the beach—and Dimitri, a fellow diver who'd said he was going to follow her to Florida.

"You only want me to come along because I keep your clothes clean and act as a buffer when you're too softhearted to tell your latest girl that you want out," Alyson accused him as she got out of the car. Bob strode across the blacktop toward the tall, imposing condominium overlooking the Atlantic. She hurried after him, struggling to control her rising irritation.

He was a handsome man, an even six feet in height, two inches taller than she. The sun highlighted the red in their identical auburn hair. Bob's features were a masculine version of hers, and they were both richly tanned from their outdoor occupation. They had the same wide, friendly mouths, but Alyson's chin hinted at her stronger determination, and her dark-lashed eyes were a smoky sea-green, while Bob's were clear blue.

"That's partly the reason," he agreed amiably. "The other is that you know how scarce jobs are during winter. With the reverse seasons down there, this'll fill in nicely. Come on, Alyson. You know you'd feel left out if you didn't come along!" he ended persuasively as they entered the building.

Alyson looked around the foyer while Bob identified himself and his sister to the security guard. The room was decorated in white and green, with matching green bamboo-print cushions on white wicker furniture. Very attractive and very expensive, she thought —and no doubt a foretaste of the penthouse where their prospective employer lived. *Bob's* prospective employer, at least. If she went along, she suspected it would only be because Bob had asked for her, and that thought rankled. She was a damned good underwater photographer and always pulled her share of the load.

Bob had come home the day before full of enthusiasm over this new job offer, but he'd had a date and had left shortly after making his announcement. Even on the drive from Jupiter to Miami he hadn't filled her in to any significant degree, except to tell her that it was a dive over the wreck of the *Santa Teresa*. The Spanish galleon had gone down in 1634, loaded with gold and silver that was earmarked for the alarmingly drained treasury in Spain. The subject had then changed to Spanish history, and Alyson never did get any further particulars about the job, other than that the man financing the venture was named Ivan Kyriokos.

Alyson had an immediate mental picture of a swarthy, heavyset millionaire who enjoyed fat, expensive cigars. Most Greeks were not particularly tall. Even Dimitri barely matched her five feet ten inches, and he was considered tall.

The guard led them to a bank of elevators. They entered the cubicle while he reached in, pushed the correct button and wished them a good day.

"Who is this Ivan Kyriokos?" Alyson asked as they glided silently upward. While Bob hadn't put it into words, Alyson knew the invitation to have lunch with Mr. Kyriokos had been set up so that he could inspect her and find out why her brother insisted she accompany him on the dive.

"I don't really know," Bob admitted, unconcerned. "I gather that he's into shipping—that is, the import and export end of it. The only thing that I'm interested in is whether there's enough financial backing to see the project through. I don't want us to be caught short the way we were on the last job." She knew that the aborted assignment still irritated him. One couldn't help becoming personally involved in a dive, and it was frustrating to leave before a project was successfully concluded.

"It's an odd combination of names," she persisted.

"His father was Greek and I think his mother was Russian. In fact, I heard somewhere that she was a princess." Bob grinned upon seeing her surprise and explained. "I was down at the Dive Shop, and you know how anything related to a new search soon becomes common knowledge."

The elevater came to a halt and the door whispered open. When they stepped into the hallway a short, swarthy man with black eyes that reminded Alyson of Greek olives greeted them. His accent was reminiscent of Dimitri's. Ivan Kyriokos, Alyson decided with some satisfaction, was exactly as she had pictured him.

They followed him down a short corridor and into the living room. The subdued elegance of the decor, framed by a breathtaking view of the ocean, made Alyson start.

Sheer curtains billowed beside sliding glass doors and drew Alyson's attention to a man standing by the balcony, silhouetted against the clear blue sky. The breath left her lungs when, as if from a great distance, she heard the short man announce them to their host.

Ivan Kyriokos stood before them, tall and slender, and Alyson's heart tripped in double time as his ebony eyes met hers. His hair was a matte black and, in deference to its tight curl, was trimmed close. It was the long, curly lashes that produced the velvety look in his dark eyes, she decided in an abstract daze. His face was narrow, with pronounced cheekbones that made his remarkable eyes slant slightly and, with the aquiline nose, hinted at his aristocratic Russian heritage. The classic jawline, however, indicated which part of his complex background was dominant.

Her gaze lingered uncontrollably on his mouth. The deep indentation in the upper curve told of a sensuality at which she could only guess. Yet, there was also a hint of cruelty, which confused her, and she tore her eyes from the disturbing sight.

Accustomed as she was to the brawny bodies of the divers she associated with, his shape seemed at first glance to be too slender until he moved forward to greet them. His stride was one of fluid grace, reminding her of a rapier: slim and deceptively beautiful when at rest; yet, a lethal weapon when used aggressively. The analogy sent a fine tremor down her spine.

"O'Hare." He nodded to her brother even as his eyes continued their examination of her face. "And you are Alyson, the twin without whom he's a man minus an arm."

Although the faint accent was pleasing, Alyson was momentarily disconcerted by the odd comparison he made. "I wouldn't go quite that far," she replied with commendable composure. "We do, however, work well together as a team and, as a result, offer more to a job than we would as individuals."

She may as well get in the sales pitch now while she had the chance. Bob, she knew, ached to go to Ecuador. While she was slightly annoyed that he'd insisted on including her, she could understand his desire to explore the new waters.

"You must have a new picture taken of yourself for your next book," Ivan said, his long, slender fingers indicating a copy of their most recent work, which was lying on a low coffee table. A manila folder with their names on it lay next to it. Alyson felt an unpleasant jolt upon realizing that he had a dossier on them, then shrugged the thought aside when he continued: "You're much more attractive than your picture."

Alyson didn't hide her amusement at his overt flattery. Did he think it would affect her? "I've no intention of entering a beauty pageant," she replied, recalling when the photo had been taken. She'd just emerged from a dive, her hair slicked back against her head and her skin sparkling with clinging drops of water. Her face mask had been pushed to the top of her head.

She didn't know why the publishers had preferred it, not realizing how her smile caught the viewer's attention. It was wide with the joy of discovery. In her hand she held a piece of coral glinting with an embedded cluster of gold doubloons. Remembering the thrill of that discovery, her mouth softened into the same enchanting curve.

Ivan's eyes narrowed slightly, their velvet warmth reaching out to encircle her. Her pulse hammered at the curve of her neck and her smile faded as she instinctively placed her hand there to hide it. He caught the movement and a faint smile of satisfaction touched the corners of his mouth.

The fact that he was aware of his power to disconcert her further unraveled her composure, and she turned abruptly to stare out the window. "You have a spectacular view, Mr. Kyriokos."

"Its attraction lies in its changeability. Do you mind heights, Alyson? If not, would you like to have a drink out on the balcony?"

He moved closer—too close; she could actually feel his body heat, and she instinctively took a step away, aware of the need to withdraw from his overwhelming presence. It was a gesture of self-preservation, and that realization momentarily stunned her.

Mercifully he turned his attention to her brother, giving her time to pull herself together. "Scotch again?" he asked, then nodded to the servant waiting at the bar to fix their drinks.

Alyson was better able to cope when he turned to her once more. "And what is your preference?" he asked.

A double Scotch was what her nerves needed, but she wisely asked for a Campari and soda. With this man she'd need every sense alert. Glasses in hand, they moved to the balcony, where he motioned for her to sit on a cushioned patio settee. The melodious chime of the doorbell brought a fleeting frown to his dark brow. An unexpected visitor, Alyson surmised, noting his reaction.

She knew she'd guessed right when Ivan's eyes frosted over as a stunning blond woman appeared at the glass door.

"Darling! I didn't know you had company. And here I am, hoping to entice you into inviting me out for lunch!" she announced gaily, then hesitated upon seeing his cold expression. She raised the eyeglass case she held as if in apology. "I left this behind last night and Giorgio kindly found it for me," she continued in a more subdued voice.

Alyson caught a glimpse of the servant standing apprehensively behind her. The woman had evidently swept by him.

"A phone call would have been sufficient, Sharon. I would have sent them over." Ivan said quietly. Taking the woman's arm, he ushered her across the living room to the door.

Alyson couldn't help hearing the woman's voice raised in a petulant question: "You will call me, won't you, darling?" But she missed Ivan's muffled answer and met Bob's amused smile with one of her own. She always thought the label that the Greeks gave to the Sharons of the world very apropos. It appeared that Ivan's "pillow friend" had made a poorly thought-out move that wasn't likely to be forgiven.

2

Resentment surged through Alyson at their host's treatment of the woman. The decent thing would have been to introduce Sharon to her and Bob. If Kyriokos had thought enough of her to bed her, the least he could have done was to extend that common courtesy —not that they'd ever meet again. Instead he'd shown her indifferently to the door as though she mattered little to him as a person. Is that what he thought of women after they'd gratified him? The thought was unpleasant.

Ivan returned shortly and picked up his drink. He took a long swallow before resuming his conversation with Bob as though nothing had happened, at the same time moving to sit beside Alyson on the settee. Only then did she see the faint outline of a lipsticked kiss on his strong jaw. Perversely desiring to chalk one up for her sex, Alyson pulled a tissue from her purse and, carefully keeping a blank expression, reached out to remove the stain.

She had to admire how quickly Ivan controlled his initial start of surprise and submitted to her ministrations. "You should warn your friends not to leave their calling cards behind," Alyson murmured audaciously, feeling a private satisfaction at being able to goad him.

He captured her hand and pressed it against the lean lines of his cheek before nipping the tip of one finger. She caught her breath, recognizing both the warning and the seduction of his action. Her gaze swung to her brother to find, thankfully, that he was staring at the ocean, oblivious to the byplay between her and Ivan.

Giorgio stepped to the door to announce lunch. Still retaining his hold on her hand, Ivan drew Alyson to her feet. "Come. I hope you'll like what Giorgio has prepared. I'm afraid he's partial to Greek food."

"We did a dive off Skyros several years ago and we both fell in love with it," Bob admitted.

"That's one of the side pleasures of our work," Alyson added, determined to act unconcerned.

Ivan hadn't released her hand; instead he'd tucked it under his arm as he led the way to the dining alcove. Determined to hold on to her composure, Alyson focused her attention on her surroundings. The dramatic elegance of the white walls and plush midnight-blue rug was certainly eye-catching. Opulently cushioned white and blue furniture were accented by large bowls of yellow- and copper-colored flowers on low tables. Masses of greenery placed in strategic corners flanked handsome marble statues of mythical Greek gods and goddesses, giving the perfect finishing touch to the lovely room. When seating her, Ivan's hands lingered for a fraction of a moment on her shoulders. The warm weight of his touch was like a fiery brand against her skin. Her composure was further shaken when he fingered the slender silver chain around her neck.

"An interesting pendant," he murmured, bending closer to examine it. "A two-real piece, isn't it?" he added, correctly identifying the Spanish coin.

Alyson nodded, trying to deny the effect he was having on her. If she raised her hand, she'd be able to satisfy her longing to feel the texture of his tightly curled hair, and was appalled at her desire. "It's one Bob found. He had it mounted on a chain and gave it to me as a present."

Glad to have a diversion for her overreacting senses, she plunged on. "I've always been intrigued by the story behind these rough-cut silver coins. Slaves pounded the metal into flat discs, which were then weighed for accuracy. Pieces were then nipped off until they were the proper weight. As a result, no two coins ever had the same appearance. Smaller denominations were made by cutting them into quarters or eighths, which is why they were called 'pieces of eight.' It's also where our slang expression *two bits*, or a quarter, came from—from two bits of an eight-real coin. She stopped abruptly, feeling like a fool. She was dithering over information he must already know.

"Very interesting," Ivan murmured, a faint smile touching his lips. His eyes caressed the gleaming wedge of silver, lingering for a second on the velvety skin against which it lay. Only when he took his seat did his gaze return to her face. Unnerved by his intense expression, Alyson lowered her eyes to concentrate on the beautifully laid table. Rich blue mats were spread across the marble top. The silverware was embossed with a meandros, a square-shaped coil, and the fine white china was adorned with the same design in a wide gold border. In the center of each plate were the entwined initials *I, D* and *K*, painted in blue.

"They were a gift," Ivan explained, noticing her interest. "Giorgio admires them, so I indulge his use of them."

"Is the *D* Greek?" she asked, wondering if his father insisted on that after allowing his wife to give Ivan his Russian first name.

"Yes. It's Dionysus."

Catching the reflexive tightening of his lips, Alyson was suddenly curious to know what lay behind the small gesture. While she placed the name as belonging to one of the Greek gods of Olympus, she was unable to recall the exact story.

With the entrance of the first course the conversation turned to favorite Greek meals that they'd enjoyed. Relieved at the introduction of a safe, impersonal topic, Alyson found herself relaxing for the first time. Lulled by Ivan's easy manners, she confided her fondness for *dolmades* and complimented Giorgio's version of the grape-leaf-wrapped concoction of deliciously spiced vegetables and meat. After the meal was over, they returned to the balcony for coffee. Alyson joined Ivan in having the strong black brew that she'd acquired a taste for when in Greece, while Bob admitted that he preferred American coffee.

"Has your brother told you the background of the *Santa Teresa*?" Ivan questioned while replenishing their cups.

Alyson breathed a sigh of relief at his evident intention to turn to the business at hand. She glanced at the two men seated around the small glass-top table. This time she was determined to resist the alluring effect that Ivan had on her senses. No matter how breathtaking the view or how lovely the open-air setting, she would keep her mind on their reason for being there.

She nodded. "From what Bob has told me, I gather that it left Peru loaded with silver and gold and sank in a storm on the Chanduy Reefs off Ecuador. Have you evidence that anything is left down there and that it's the *Teresa* you've spotted? I've read how they trained the Indians to dive. The boat could have been stripped."

Ivan's dark brows arched at the temerity of her question. "I do not expend the large amount of capital on a venture like this without first thoroughly researching the project."

Silenced by his caustic rebuff, Alyson lowered her eyes. She deserved the put-down. It was unthinkable that he did not do his homework carefully.

"Your question does have merit," Ivan amended in a slightly less harsh tone, his irritation under quick control. "My men researched the history of this ship as completely as possible. The facts are clear: Yes, slaves were brought down from Mexico after the vessel went down. Records show that they retrieved only a small portion of the sunken cargo before winter set in and they had to stop. When they returned the following year, the shifting currents had covered the wreck so thoroughly that they were unable to recover anything more, even though the ship had settled in little more than thirty feet of water."

While Ivan's voice had gentled slightly, his face still held an austere expression, a warning that he was not used to being questioned. Too bad, Alyson thought truculently. Her error was in forgetting that she wasn't just chatting with one of her co-workers.

Ivan leaned back in his chair, his fingers tapping a light tattoo on the tabletop while he regarded her. "Quite frankly, Alyson, you present a problem. I need your brother, but I don't know if there's a place for you in this project. I thought I had my team all selected until one of my divers had to cancel at the last minute. I'm lucky to have found a substitute of your brother's caliber. You must know the logistics of this type of effort. There's no room for an unnecessary person."

Alyson's eyes sparked with instant anger. "If you had had your much-vaunted research team check with my past employers, you'd have found that I've never been 'unnecessary.' I've always pulled my full load. As it happens, I have other commitments and was only going along to accommodate my brother." She rose abruptly, hoping that her trembling was undetectable. How dare he think she'd join an expedition as a tagalong!

"Alyson!" Bob rose to his feet, his expression reflecting his surprise. Seldom did his usually unflappable sister display so much temper.

"Sit down, both of you!" Ivan commanded.

They sat down under the force of the order. Had she really thought that his eyes were like velvet? she wondered, noting the glitter of anger in their black depths.

"Miss O'Hare, it would help if you would allow me to finish," he continued. "Are you always so quick to jump to conclusions?" He ignored her gasp of outrage. "Your brother has listed your qualifications and they have already been verified."

Her head snapped up. So the folder on the coffee

table did hold a dossier on them! He must have access to a formidable research team if they'd already presented him with material on her. The thought of such an invasion of her privacy was repellent.

"You mean you had us investigated?" she demanded icily.

Ivan's expression underscored the redundancy of the question. "I am, first of all, a businessman, Miss O'Hare. And in a case such as this, in which money other than mine is involved, I naturally check very carefully the qualifications of those on whom the success of the mission depends. You were invited here so that we could lay the groundwork for the dive and get your input on what special supplies you wish ordered."

Alyson hadn't blushed since childhood, but she couldn't suppress the embarrassment that sent a heat wave scorching her cheeks. Ever since arriving she'd felt as if her equilibrium had slipped a little off center—all because of the effect this man had on her. "I'm sorry," she murmured contritely.

"*Ehé!* It is partly my fault," he admitted in exasperation. "Sometimes the words come out wrong when I speak in another language while thinking in Greek."

Alyson looked up upon hearing his explanation, her taut muscles slowly relaxing. The velvet was back in his eyes. Surprised by how relieved she felt, she acknowledged his apology with a tiny nod.

"So! Shall we have another cup of coffee and continue with the discussion?" He flicked a long finger and Alyson obediently refilled the cups from silver pots that Giorgio had placed on the side table—and wondered over her compliance as she did so. She would let his bossiness slide by this time, deciding that she'd caused enough argument. His condescending attitude reminded her of his treatment of his unexpected guest. For a moment she had forgotten his unpalatable opinion of her sex. More than ever, she wished Bob would agree to her staying behind on this dive.

"I now have a full complement of divers," Ivan began. "But I'm well aware how accidents can happen. Do you have the knowledge to take one of their places if necessary?"

Bob answered for her, unexpectedly protective. Alyson barely listened as he enumerated her qualifications as a photographer as well as an amateur archaeologist. Instead she tried to think of an acceptable way to stay home. She couldn't remember feeling so awkward before in her life, or being so totally aware of a man whom she had just met. Neither reaction pleased her, and every instinct warned her to cut and run.

"The main problem that you present is where to bed you, Miss O'Hare." Ivan's choice of words effectively pulled Alyson from her mental wanderings. By the amused glint in his eye, she knew her reaction had been deliberately triggered.

"I've rented a small villa on the shore off the Chanduy Reefs. The second floor is open and will be used as the men's dormitory. There's one bedroom on the first floor, but it's assigned to the captain of the salvage ship and his wife, who will be your cook." He paused for a second, his glance sardonic. "Of course, the men will sleep mostly on the ship. But it will be a long summer and there'll be times when they'll be ashore. I'll be frank. There will be little chance for them to get into town, and you're an attractive woman. I hope that you'll see that it doesn't become a problem."

Hot words rose, but his expression made her drop her lashes to shield her anger. Had his researchers dug up stories about Dimitri? she wondered as she refused to dignify his statement with a reply. She had to admit in all honesty that she had faced such accusations before, although they had been couched in more subtle words. Bob was looking at her with open amusement. He knew how she was squirming.

Ivan continued. "However, there is a shed on the grounds that I plan to turn into a developing lab. Since you'll be placed in charge of it, space could be set aside for a bed. That is, unless you prefer we set up a tent for you."

There was an unexpected challenge in his eyes, which she answered quickly. "The shed will be fine." From experience she knew it would be vastly preferable to have a solid roof over her head.

He nodded as if secretly pleased, but before the thought could settle, he went on. "I planned to check the salvage boat this afternoon. Would you like to come along? You may have some suggestions."

"Is it being outfitted here in Miami?" Bob asked, perking up with interest. On being told the name of the marina, which was nearby, he confessed his eagerness to see the boat.

Alyson found herself sitting between the two men in Ivan's Lincoln Continental. They threaded their way through the crowded streets to the boatyard, which faced a wide stretch of Biscayne Bay. It proved to be a small working marina rather than one catering to visiting yachtsman.

Various boats, mostly shrimpers and charter vessels, were being repaired. The yard was busy, the air filled with the wine of power tools and the thud of hammers.

Bright flashes indicated where acetylene torches were in use.

They were led to a craft that was about ninety feet long. It was an old craft, but the lovely sleek lines marked it as once having been someone's pleasure yacht. A ladder leaned against the hull, and Ivan suggested that Bob go first. "Just to make certain it's safe on deck for your sister," he added, raising his voice above the din.

Alyson questioned the purity of his motive when halfway up her sandaled shoe slipped on one of the rungs. A strong hand encircled her calf, placing her foot on the proper step. She was left wondering if it was only by accident that the long fingers had explored her ankle caressingly for an instant. For some unknown reason a picture of the sensuous outline of Ivan's mouth flashed through her mind, bringing a new wave of the trembling he'd evoked so easily in her earlier. She reached for Bob's steadying hand as she stepped over the gunwale and onto the comparative safety of the deck.

The place would have been a mass of confusion to an inexperienced eye. Parts littered the deck while busy workmen hurried about their tasks. Alyson noted the two powerful winches that were being bolted to the deck. Those would control the life lines to the divers below, haul up the heavier objects recovered and be ready in case of trouble to assist the divers.

Bob and Alyson were impressed by the nearly completed renovation. This was no hit-or-miss affair. From the advanced radar and telecommunications systems to the stainless-steel galley, the entire operation showed careful attention to detail. Even the bunks were better than usual, being large enough for someone of Bob's size. Since the divers would remain on board during their off-duty hours, this was an added luxury.

Alyson waited patiently while her brother examined the make of the air compressors for the diving tanks and the various gear already assembled. He was in his element, his expression reflecting his pleasure. She knew that mentally he was already anticipating testing the equipment on his first dive into the waters off Ecuador.

Not for the first time she equated Bob with the explorers whose ship they were salvaging—men who had pushed into new frontiers, driven by an unknown force that urged them ever on. She should be grateful to men like Ivan Kyriokos who made his quest possible. Until now she usually was.

Her gaze swept over Ivan, his aristocratic head bent slightly, his black brows pulled into a frown while concentrating on a blueprint the foreman was explaining to him. Somehow gratitude wasn't the feeling he aroused in her. She admitted to being thankful that after today there'd be little likelihood of meeting him again.

When Ivan and Bob were finished, the three descended the ladder and walked around the boat while Bob exclaimed enthusiastically over the renovations.

"You've put a lot of thought into the outfitting, Mr. Kyriokos," Alyson complimented him sincerely.

"Ivan," he corrected her. "I think by now we have progressed to a first-name basis, hmm?"

His eyes roved evaluatingly over her, causing Alyson to turn away to study the boat. She focused on the stern and the unusual name painted across the transom. *"Semele,"* she remarked, testing the strange name against her tongue. She turned to the tall man beside her as recognition came. "Wasn't she one of your goddesses?"

Ivan's lips tightened slightly, as they had when she'd questioned about his middle name. "No," he returned abruptly. "She was the only mortal Zeus ever loved, but eventually she was permitted to live on Olympus."

When in Skyros, Alyson had become interested in Greek mythology and had bought several books on the lusty and somewhat terrifying adventures of the legendary gods of ancient Greece. She strove to recall the details of Semele's story, but Bob interrupted with a question about the projected date for the boat to start south.

"As you can see, they're almost finished here. It should be in the water in a few days. The Savilles, the captain and his wife, have already ordered what is to be taken along. If the schedule holds up, the *Semele* should be sailing in two weeks."

"Are we supposed to go with them?" Bob questioned.

"Why, are you offering your services? Bill will need only a skeleton crew. The rest of you will fly down after the boat arrives."

Bob glanced at Alyson questioningly. "I've never sailed through the Panama Canal," he admitted, his longing evident.

"Why don't you go," Alyson urged, accepting the broad hint. "Without you around I could get the book finished up." She grinned at her brother to take the sting from her words. Bob, as they both knew, was more likely to waste hours reminiscing over an interesting event than helping to select the best photos to illustrate their work.

"I'll give you Captain Bill's phone number," Ivan

offered agreeably, "and leave it to you to see about making arrangements."

When they left, it was Ivan who held her elbow with his long, slender fingers, who splayed his hand across the small of her back to guide her over the strands of cable crisscrossing the yard. A smile tugged on her lips when he hurried her past the workmen, who took time out to look her over. He acted as possessive as she remembered Dimitri had. Was it an inbred trait of Greek men to behave this way with women who happened to interest them?

Bob was quiet during the ride home. It was so at odds with her brother's usual talkativeness when contemplating a new enterprise that Alyson kept glancing curiously his way.

"All right, what's bothering you?" she demanded finally when he turned off I-95 to pick up the road to their home in Jupiter.

He hunched over the wheel and frowned through the windshield before answering. "I was thinking maybe it would be better for you to stay here this winter and work on that book you've set your heart on. I have no right to try to change your mind."

Alyson had lived too long on her twin's wavelength not to sense that he was hedging. The question was why and about what. "Oh, I don't know," she murmured casually. "I'd like to see something of Ecuador. Ivan's put a lot of research behind this venture and it could pan out."

The frown grew heavier. "Since when are you on a first-name basis with him?"

Her eyes widened in surprise. "Since he asked me. What are you so uptight about?"

"I don't want you to have anything to do with that man!" Bob said forcefully.

"Are you assuming on the basis of this one visit that he'd want me for a 'pillow friend'?" she questioned archly.

A red flush surged up his neck. "Come off it, Alyson. I saw the way he watched you. He's already figuring out how long it will take to get you in his bed."

So it hadn't been her imagination! "I don't believe what I'm hearing," she countered with a mocking laugh while denying the shiver of awareness that danced down her spine. "I seem to recall an assortment of women who happened to join us for breakfast and even bunked in for a while. Since we have only two bedrooms, and I've never shared mine with them, I wonder where they slept."

Their bedrooms were on opposite ends of the condominium, and after the surprised shock of the first time, she'd accepted the situation with a shrug. After all, he owned half the apartment, and the women for the most part were pleasant.

He glanced at her from the corner of his eye. "Do you object? You've never said anything."

"Heavens, no!" Alyson protested. "We might live and work together, but we don't live in each other's pocket. But don't forget, brother dear, like you, I'm twenty-eight years old."

Bob gestured impatiently. "But this man is way out of your league. You could be hurt."

"Bob, don't you think you're making a big thing out of nothing?" she asked with forced lightness. The atmosphere was too heavy and she wanted to clear the air. "I probably won't see him again anyway. We'll be in Ecuador, and Lord knows where he'll be."

Silenced by her statement of the obvious, Bob stared straight ahead. Alyson gazed resolutely out the window in an effort to banish the memory of the sensations that she'd felt when Ivan's strong, slender fingers had encircled her ankle with a caressing touch.

Ivan, complicated, elegant and sophisticated, filled her mind. He had tantalized her senses, rocked her composure and awakened feelings never before aroused. And if Bob was right, Ivan wanted her.

3

~~~~~~~~~~~~~~~

Alyson pursed her lips as she evaluated the merits of the photos lined up on the dining table. She glanced at her brother, who was sprawled in his favorite position on the sofa. His bare feet were propped on the coffee table as he examined the pages of a catalog of scuba diving equipment.

A small sigh of frustration escaped from her lips. It was useless to ask for his help until she pared the latest batch down to the best three or four. Then she'd wait for him to make a remark about one that caught his eye. The ploy was frequently used as a way of making her final decision. She figured that if a picture appealed to him regardless of how skillfully it was composed, then it would do the same for the viewing public. So far her odd formula had been successful.

"Do they have a sale on fins?" she asked, suddenly remembering that she needed a new pair. "The heels on the last ones never felt quite as comfortable as they should."

"I'll add it to the list. Bill asked me to check out what the divers would need and see if they had missed out on anything."

"Bill?"

Bob squirmed a second before answering defiantly. "Bill Saville, the captain of the *Semele*. I gave him a call and one thing led to another."

Alyson moved before him, hands on hips. "Bob O'Hare, sometimes I could cheerfully wring your neck!" she cried in exasperation. He'd been oddly reticent about the Ecuador venture ever since their return from Miami two days before. Until that slip he'd made no mention of contacting the captain. She felt more than a mere neck-wringing was in order. "Well, tell me, are you crewing for him?"

"Yes," he admitted meekly, "along with another diver, the radioman and an engineer to keep those diesels running."

"I hope you have rough weather all the way!" she seethed.

Seeing her annoyance, he grinned. "The *Semele* looks like she can take anything. And while you're standing there, doing nothing, how about starting lunch? I'm starving."

She felt like telling him what he could do with his lunch when he mused aloud: "That's an odd name— *Semele*. I wonder if it's named after someone in Ivan's family."

Alyson recalled her intention of investigating that same question in her mythology books and turned to search for them on the bookshelves. Lunch was forgotten as her curiosity took over.

"Here it is," she announced a few minutes later,

after flipping through the pages of one volume. "Dionysus, Greek god of vegetation and wine, and . . . oh! . . . son of Zeus and Semele," she read to him. "That's where he got the name! This is interesting," she added as she continued reading. "Semele was the only mortal whom Zeus ever loved, but she was burned to ashes through trickery by his jealous wife. Zeus plucked their unborn son from her and sewed him to his thigh until he was ready to be born. How about that! Later Dionysus went to Hades and rescued his mother and persuaded the gods to let her live as an immortal on Olympus. And get this! Bacchus is the Roman name for Dionysus."

"The god of orgies and debauchery," Bob muttered darkly. "He may be more aptly named than you think. Stay away from him, Alyson!"

"Now who's being silly?" she laughed as she went to the kitchen to create the lavish sandwich that was her twin's favorite. What was the connection between that fable and the naming of the ship? she wondered. Had she imagined Ivan's tensing when questioned? She shrugged the questions away and added another slice of provolone cheese to the many-layered submarine sandwich.

Alyson admitted to being amused and somewhat touched by Bob's protectiveness where the Greek magnate was concerned. While Ivan had intrigued her, she was certain that their meeting had been the one and only they'd have. Naturally he'd want to see who he was hiring, especially considering his reservation about adding a woman to his crew.

She was busy typing a running commentary to accompany the photos chosen for the book when the phone rang. Bob, returning from a jaunt somewhere, scooped up the receiver in his large hand and growled a hello. He shot a look at his sister and hunched his shoulders as he turned his back to her. Hearing the low rumble of his voice, Alyson smiled wryly. A new girl, no doubt. But why hide the fact?

Bob returned the phone to the cradle before turning to her. "That was Kyriokos," he said brusquely.

"And?" she returned sharply. Really, he was carrying the watchful-brother routine too far!

"He's having the captain and his wife over tomorrow at three to do a final check on the supply lists. Since Bill handed me the problem of outfitting the divers, he wants me there too."

"Oh." Alyson turned to the typewriter, not realizing the disappointment evident in that one word. "Well, don't forget to take all your catalogs along."

"He wants you, too."

Seeing his scowl, Alyson shook her head in exasperation. "For heaven's sake, will you stop gnawing on that bone? You saw the type of woman that appeals to him. Would you ever compare me with Sharon? Now, tell me why he wants me along; I'll bet it's a perfectly logical reason."

Bob grinned sheepishly. "You win. I'll stop acting the heavy. Ivan has a list of supplies he's ordered for the photo lab. Since you're now in charge of that department, he suggested you come along to see that you have everything that you'll need."

Alyson was unable to stop the warmth invading her. "Since the meeting is so late, how about staying in Miami for the evening? You owe me a dinner in one of those fancy restaurants after these past few weeks of cooking for you." Her mind was already racing ahead. She could wear that super dress that she'd bought on a whim. It was a bit dressy for just a meal with her brother, but every woman needed to get dressed up once in a while, she consoled herself.

The next day Alyson was in a state of excited anticipation. Try as she would, she was unable to banish Ivan's image from her mind. A purely feminine desire to be her dazzling best had taken over.

She spent a delightful half hour relaxing in a hot perfumed bath before shampooing her hair. She knew that most men preferred long hair, but of necessity she wore a more practical close cut. She'd been on too many locations where fresh water was at a premium, and nothing felt worse than lank, salt-laden hair. When dry, the short style brushed easily into a sophisticated cap of shining auburn waves.

Since the design of the newly purchased dress precluded the wearing of a bra, Alyson slipped into lacy mocha bikini pants and a matching half-slip, both fetching against the golden tan she'd acquired in Sicily.

Alyson paused to run her hand over her dress, enjoying the sensual pleasure the velvety textured material produced. The ultrasuede crepe was a designer's dream, hugging her body with a subtle sexuality. The richness of its café au lait was a perfect complement to her sun-kissed skin.

The cross-draped bodice lovingly molded the soft swell of her breasts. The multiple strands of gold chains gleaming softly against her throat only momentarily halted the glide of discerning eyes to the deep vee neckline. The slim side wrap of the skirt ended in a slit down her left thigh. The gently rounded hem produced a fragile tulip effect that was dispelled the moment the wearer moved or sat. Then the skirt parted slightly to reveal a fetching portion of slender leg to the appreciative viewer.

Of course it was too dressy for the projected meeting, so Alyson slipped on the companion jacket and fastened the row of tiny cloth-covered buttons to create a more demure neckline. But there again the designer had sought to draw attention to the woman's femininity. The conventional straight sleeves ended in a four-inch slit and repeated the tulip curve of the hem. Any movement of her arm gave unexpected and therefore enticing glimpses of the golden link bracelets at her wrists.

Her brother's impatient call reached her as she made one final check of her reflection in the mirror. She'd matched the bronze tone of her nail polish in her lipstick. Her eye makeup held a blended touch of aquamarine that echoed the sea green of her irises. With a last approving look at her image, Alyson left her bedroom.

Bob's first reaction was an appreciative whistle, which quickly turned into a suspicious scowl. "Who are you dressing up for?" he demanded sharply.

"For you, little brother, who else?" she replied, not quite truthfully. Slipping her arm through his, she urged him to the door. "It's been such a long time since we've been out together without dates that I thought we'd make an occasion of it." She squeezed his arm companionably before leaving him to lock up while she walked to the car.

When they first bought their quarter of the building, she'd had her doubts about the privacy afforded by the design. The fenced-in patio had proved surprisingly efficient. The lure of the setup had been that they were able to lock the door and not worry about maintenance when going off on a job. She and Bob knew they wouldn't be happy in a high-rise, and this had turned out to be a suitable substitute for a privately owned home.

It was a beautiful October day, with a lingering summer's warmth that was typical of Florida's sub-tropical climate. The car's speed created enough breeze to keep Alyson comfortable in the jacketed dress. They were so accustomed to living and working outdoors that they seldom resorted to air conditioning.

"Are you getting the equipment you requested?" she asked, admitting to feeling annoyed over being kept in the dark about the progress of the expedition. The divers' requirements always held priority, she knew, since the success of any salvage operation depended upon their mobility. If there was to be any budget-pinching, it would be done in such areas as photography.

"Nothing has been crossed off the list. Of course, today may prove that the blue pencil's been at work."

"Is the work on the *Semele* on schedule?" Alyson had tried, with minimal success, to picture how the once beautiful luxury yacht had looked before being outfitted for the search.

"Bill said it's in the water. There were only a few minor details left to finish."

"Then you'll meet the target date next week?"

Bob nodded. "It can't come too soon for me," he admitted with a familiar sigh.

Alyson laughed, having no trouble guessing the reason for his heartfelt agreement. "I warned you, little brother. What's the matter? Is the latest fling proving to be too clinging?"

Bob shot her a rueful look. "After last night, I can't wait to get to Ecuador."

"One of these days you'll learn where to draw the line," Alyson reprimanded him gently. "You're a good-looking man in what most women think is a glamorous profession. It adds up to a very provocative package."

"The problem is that I'm a pushover for soft, cuddly objects," he shot back, doing a little teasing of his own.

"Since when do you call women objects?" she protested, ready for battle.

He flashed an easy grin in her direction, causing them both to chuckle. Bob turned the car into Ivan's parking lot and the light exchange faded, to be replaced by the unnerving tension that invaded Alyson whenever her thoughts strayed to the tall Greek.

"Doesn't Ivan have a separate office?" she asked as the elevator carried them to the top floor.

"I think he's in Miami now only because of this venture," Bob hazarded. "The first time I came, we met in the study. I guess he uses that as his office while he's here."

Giorgio's black eyes were warm in greeting. He led them to a side door off the corridor that she hadn't noticed during her first visit. The study was another attractive room, but it faced west, overlooking the busy intracoastal waterway. Ivan's love for statuary marble was again in evidence with a beautifully sculptured nude woman placed in one corner of the window so that she seemed to be staring pensively at the water below.

Alyson's gaze took in Ivan, sitting behind a handsome leather-topped desk, and three strangers in the room. A square-set, iron-gray haired man, obviously ill at ease in his business suit, was introduced as

Captain Bill Saville. Elsa, his wife and the expedition's cook, was a plump, motherly-looking woman who smiled warmly at her.

The third person was a slender, dark-haired, dark-eyed man who proved to be Ivan's secretary. He advised them with a white-toothed smile to call him Sylvos instead of his tortuously complicated last name. "Only another Greek could hope to get it correct," he added.

When they sat down, Sylvos arranged several folders neatly before Ivan, after which he retreated to a chair in the background. His hand poised over a pad, he waited for the meeting to continue. Apparently the captain and his wife had already finished their report.

Alyson listened as Ivan went over Bob's list with him. He checked what was already on hand and the probability of the rest being delivered by sailing time. They were trying to avoid having to send the missing items by expensive airfreight to Ecuador.

"And you, Alyson—are you satisfied with what's been ordered for your work?"

The deep, slightly accented voice brought her attention to him. The top buttons on his white linen sport shirt were open, and the shadowing cast by his olive skin indicated that he wore no undershirt. A light dusting of hair was evident on his chest. She had an aversion to hirsute men and was pleased with him. The intruding sensations were quickly pushed aside. This was a business meeting, she reminded herself sternly.

"I would know if I had a list," she replied to his question.

A sharp hiss escaped from between Ivan's teeth as he eyed his secretary with cold disapproval. Sylvos quickly extracted a sheet of paper from the sheaf he held and hurried to hand it to her.

"My apologies, Miss O'Hare. I thought this had gone out to you," he murmured as he slid an apprehensive glance at the thin-lipped man behind the desk.

Ivan Kyriokos was not one to tolerate such slips, Alyson was certain. She gave the secretary a reassuring smile. "If you'll give me five minutes, I'll be able to give you an answer."

"Ehê!" Ivan said, causing Alyson to smile in recognition of his repeated use of that versatile Greek expression. A shift of emphasis could change it from a sign of simple irritation to one of deep disgust. "It's time for a coffee break." He flicked a long finger, and a chastened Sylvos left hurriedly to carry out the order.

Giorgio entered within minutes, carrying a large silver tray holding two silver pots and china in what she recognized as her favorite Limoges pattern. Evidently remembering her appreciation of the stronger Greek coffee, he poured hers without asking her preference. Only Ivan and she drank the stronger brew, she noticed. The others had the less potent American blend from the second pot.

While sipping from the fragile cup, Alyson was aware that the man who dominated the room was watching her. He lifted his cup fractionally in a silent toast before raising it to his lips. It was a barely noticeable gesture, one only she could have seen. She was left with the disconcerting feeling that she was being stroked with velvet gloves. The sensations produced were ones she preferred to keep hidden, but she suspected that he knew her reaction.

Darn the man! she swore with an odd combination

of amusement and resentment. This was not the time or place to play his little game. This was a business meeting. She wasn't about to let him see how she was reacting to his little ploy.

"I don't know much about Ecuador," she said calmly. "I do know that the equator runs through it, but is it hot and humid where we'll be stationed? Will I need an air conditioner for the shed? Mildew can quickly ruin the film."

"Where you'll be stationed you'll find it similar to what we have here in Florida. As you know, the water is kept cool by the Peruvian Current, which affects the coastal climate."

"That's why I've ordered foam-insulated wet suits," Bob inserted.

Alyson nodded. There'd be no delightfully refreshing swims at midnight, as she'd experienced in Sicily. The thought triggered memories of Dimitri, and for a moment she was disconcerted that she had difficulty recalling his features. It had been, after all, another romance that had faded with distance, she conceded resignedly.

"I can't see any necessary additions," Alyson reported after carefully checking the items listed. "If we do run short of film, I imagine we can buy some in Guayaquil."

Ivan agreed as he closed the files on his desk. The Savilles rose at the signal that the meeting was over, and she and Bob joined them.

"Can you wait a few minutes, Bob?" Ivan asked after saying his good-byes to the captain and his wife. "I hope you can supply information about some divers that I need. Or will it be holding you from an important date?" Bob was dressed in eye-catching red slacks and a navy jacket. Coupled with her smart outfit, it made it obvious that they were contemplating a night out after the meeting.

"It's nothing pressing," Bob said with his easy grin. "Alyson talked me into trying a restaurant in this area and I'm being the dutiful brother."

"This won't take long," Ivan promised. "But come, let's go into the living room, where it's more comfortable. Can I interest you in a drink?"

His long fingers curled around Alyson's elbow to guide her. He was much too close again. When in the room, she moved to take a chair, only to be led to the deep sofa.

The yellow and bronze chrysanthemums had been replaced with pots of pink and rose cyclamen, she noticed. The change of color against the stark deep blue and white gave the room a completely new look.

Ivan revealed that he was once again short a diver. The man had been checking on an outfall problem for the city of Miami and had contracted a low-grade fever that was defying every antibiotic. Since his sinuses and ears were infected, he was forced to curtail all dives for an indeterminate length of time. As in other highly specialized professions, most top divers knew each other personally or by reputation, and Ivan was hoping to rely on Bob's knowledge to help him find someone to take the missing diver's place.

As she'd anticipated, after Giorgio served their drinks, Ivan joined her on the sofa. She frowned. There was no need for him to sit so near, swamping her with his warmth and the electric charisma he exuded. He was definitely too sexually attuned for her liking. She discovered that he had enough of an effect on her to cause her to gulp down half of her Campari without thinking.

Driven by a restlessness that she couldn't understand, Alyson rose and went to the balcony. While she knew most of the divers Bob was describing, she decided to leave the men to their discussion. She leaned on the railing, enjoying the cool, refreshing breeze. The days were getting shorter and the faraway horizon was darkening as night began pulling its cover over the ocean.

Alyson had no idea how long she stood there before she heard the footfall on the hard concrete floor of the balcony. She glanced over her shoulder and breathed a sigh of relief upon seeing her brother coming toward her.

"Finished?" she asked, hurriedly draining the last of the melted ice cubes from her glass. "Have you decided where we're going? Frankly, I'm starved."

Bob looked embarrassed before taking her glass. "Ivan told me to mix you another drink while he changes. He's coming with us."

Alyson stared at him in surprise. It didn't make sense. Bob had been acting the heavy brother where Ivan was concerned, and his announcement was an unexpected turnaround.

"I made the mistake of asking him if he knew of a good Greek restaurant, and before I knew it, he insisted on taking us to one that's his favorite." Bob's expression was of rueful acceptance. His easy nature frequently caused him to take the path of least resistance. She could see how he'd be no match for the dominating Greek. The fresh drink was accepted with a sense of fatalism.

Ivan insisted they use his Lincoln, and Alyson again found herself sitting between the two men as he threaded through the traffic. Her glance slid to the aristocratic profile. She wished to look behind the controlled mask he seemed to wear. It had been in place throughout the exchange in the study; he had lowered it only momentarily while they had coffee. His visual stroking, which had warmed her with its intense sensuality, had permitted her to catch a glimpse of his softer side.

She was quite certain that if she lived closer, he'd try to get her to his bed, as her brother had warned after their first meeting. It took one wolf to recognize the hunting skills of another.

The front of the restaurant was unpretentious. However, once through the door, the mouth-watering aromas brought back memories of the small family-run taverns that they'd enjoyed on Skyros.

The rotund proprietor hurried to Ivan, his face beaming a welcome. They spoke in Greek for a few minutes, and Alyson was pleased that she could still recognize an occasional word. The health of the various members of his family was discussed, especially that of the latest baby.

"Ah, but you came to taste the delicious food, not to be bored with my family!" the man apologized as he ushered them to a corner table partially screened by potted plants.

Alyson watched, her amusement tinged with irritation as Ivan ordered without consulting them. Did he always have to take command? The annoyance quickly faded when she tasted the superlative food. The *escabeche,* white fish sauted with hot peppers and black olives, was as tasty as she remembered. The *spanakopitta* was something new, and upon inquiry Ivan explained that it was the dill and feta cheese that made the spinach baked in *phyllo* dough taste so different.

"When is the *Semele* expected to arrive in Ecuador?" she asked. Her book was coming together quicker than expected, and she hoped the first draft would be off to her publisher before she had to leave. "I need a target date to close our condo and get the plane tickets."

"I've already arranged for your ticket—the third week in November," Ivan informed her. "I'm sorry that you won't be here to celebrate your Thanksgiving. Christmas will be away from home also. We have only their three summer months to give to this venture."

"Then Bob will be on his way next week." She smiled at her brother, knowing how eager he was to start. "Who do I contact about when and where I leave?" The excitement of anticipation was building in her.

"You'll get the information in plenty of time. Just make certain the heavier equipment goes on the boat."

It made sense not to have to pay extra airfreight, and she agreed with a qualifier. "I prefer to carry my cameras, but I'll send everything else."

"Fine," Ivan said, signaling to the waiter for the check. "I have a van on order for transportation because the villa is a distance from Guayaquil, which is Ecuador's main seaport."

While waiting for the Lincoln to be brought to the door, Alyson started to ask him who the other divers were. She knew or had heard of most of the top professionals, and was wondering who she'd be associating with. Because of the nature of their work, their lives depended upon each other.

The question flew from her mind when the valet opened the door for her and Ivan ushered her into the car with fingertips that seemed to contain their own supply of electricity. Why else would her arm tingle so?

"I planned to investigate a new nightclub that has opened," Ivan announced suavely as he entered the flow of traffic. "I hear the band is exceptionally good."

As they rode, every nerve ending warned Alyson of the danger of dancing with this man. It would be sheer madness to submit to having his arm binding her close, her body aligned with his. So far she'd managed to keep ahead of the erupting thoughts that he triggered, to keep a clamp on the inner flutterings she experienced when she was near him. But since she loved dancing and was good at it, Bob would immediately suspect if she refused Ivan's request.

She shrugged off her disturbing thoughts, and when they arrived at the nightclub she concentrated on the lavish decor. The band lived up to its promise with a foot-tapping beat. Alyson felt her reservations dissolve, and her drink added to the warmth building in her. When she undid the row of small buttons on her jacket, Bob leaned forward to help her out of it. A soft hiss was expelled from between Ivan's teeth, alerting Alyson to that typical Greek expression of approval.

Bob's glance darted at her and Alyson was sorely pressed not to act the shy maiden by placing her hands over the exposed cleavage. "Maybe you better put the jacket on again," he muttered.

Ivan laughed. "You're playing the role of a protective husband!" Then his attention was caught by friends waving from another table. He excused himself to speak with them, leaving Bob to ask Alyson to dance.

"That was a silly thing to say!" she chastised her twin as he twirled her into the crowd. "Especially after the way you kept taking inventory of the woman at the next table!"

"I rest my case," he said with his irrepressible grin, leaving Alyson shaking her head in exasperation. The band moved into a disco beat, and they matched steps to the faster rhythm.

She entertained no thought of slipping on her jacket when they returned to their seats. Flushed from the exercise, she drained her highball. She watched Ivan return through silky lashes, vibrantly aware of his imposing form as he threaded his way back to their table.

He paused by her chair and extended his hand. "We have time for our dance before they put on the floor show," Ivan murmured, and once again she found herself being led to the dance floor.

"Is your brother always so protective of you?" he asked as he drew her into his arms.

"It works two ways," she answered guardedly.

"I understand that you also keep house for him, and no doubt attend to all the little housewifely details."

"I'm his twin!" she retorted sharply, wondering what he was driving at.

"And he's easygoing enough to let you continue to devote your life to assure his comforts," he said in strong reprimand. "Where is Alyson O'Hare going to be if he ever meets a strong-enough-minded woman to shake him from this comfortable setup?"

Her sea-green eyes sparked with sudden anger. "Are you inferring that I'm doing him a disservice?"

"Only you can answer that," he murmured smoothly. "But enough on that subject. Your dress is very attractive. Am I reading the message correctly?"

Her head snapped back. She glared into the dark eyes a few inches above hers. The velvety blackness had receded, allowing her to see the mocking lights of his indecision over whether or not she was worth the chase. It was a mortifying look into his mind, and her reaction was predictable.

"I don't know what message you're reading, Mr. Kyriokos," she flared, "but if you look around at the dresses on other women, mine is decidedly modest in comparison."

His glance slid over the extreme dècolletage of the nearby dancers before dropping to the shadowed V of her dress. "Which only proves my contention," he challenged. "Most women are out to sell their bodies, whether consciously or not."

"I'm certain you're speaking from vast experience," she bit out, aghast at his evaluation of her gender.

"Vast enough," he admitted with a shrug.

The horrible part was that she believed him. "I can feel sorry for you if you limit your associations to one type of woman."

"I've been known to be a generous man," he informed her with a mocking smile.

Alyson stumbled as she missed a step. How dare he assume that she'd trade her body in that manner! "I think I've had enough dancing for the night." Appalled indignation grated in her voice.

His answer was to pull her closer until their bodies were in full contact. Her senses leaped as his long thighs forced hers to move in unison with his. Once again she was made aware of the rapier strength camouflaged by his slender body. After hearing his low opinion of her sex, she tried unsuccessfully to fight the insidious reaction.

"Am I disturbing you with such frank talk?" he murmured soothingly, his accent suddenly more pronounced. "My friends periodically call me to task over it," he admitted with unexpected candor. "I didn't mean for you to take to heart what I said. Come, let us concentrate on the music. Shall we start all over? I am a man and you are a woman, and what better circumstances are there at this moment in time than for us to enjoy the delight of dancing in each other's arms?"

Alyson had no reply. He knew she wouldn't create a scene by struggling from his embrace—not that his grip would permit her to. Something in the sensuous word picture he'd painted diminished her anger. He was a superlative dancer, and the music was a dreamy rendition of an old ballad. And her body was entranced by how his body warmth invaded hers. She closed her eyes as a small sigh escaped her lips. Her tension drained away as she gave in to the seduction of the moment. There seemed something preordained about the way they blended so perfectly together, each curve finding a compatible place against the other.

Ivan's cheek rested against her forehead as he led her through the steps. "Put your arms around my neck," he murmured and she did as requested with a dreamy compliance. His hands slid over her back to rest on the curve of her hips.

"I like the feel of your dress. . . . It's like velvet." His sensitive fingers stroked the material.

It was the texture of the ultrasuede crepe that had first attracted her, and she could understand his reaction.

"I'll have to buy you a whole wardrobe of it," he breathed softly, his lips brushing warmly over her forehead. "It's like an extension of your skin. Ever since the first time I touched you I've been wanting to discover if the rest of your body has the same texture."

His husky whisper held her with its seduction. She could appreciate the line he was casting, and told herself bracingly that she should be experienced enough not to be hooked by his lure. Meanwhile, she confessed, she was thoroughly enjoying the way tingling fingers of excitement were tripping down her spine, and the sensuous claim his very sinewy body was placing on hers. He was exuding a subtle aroma that was more complex than what came from a bottle. It was a basic masculine scent, a muskiness that was causing her to lose control of her limbs. She found herself leaning against him, lost in a helpless excitement that she had never experienced before.

The warning bells were much too faint to heed.

4

It's over, dream girl," Ivan whispered into her ear. Alyson reluctantly forced her eyes open, only then realizing that the music had stopped.

He led her from the floor, her hand clasped tightly in his. It was a necessary anchor to hold down her floating body. She felt euphoric, as if she were experiencing the dangerous rapture of the deep, a condition in which divers were known to lose their reasoning powers to the extent that they sometimes removed their masks, certain that they were one with the underwater environment and could breath like fish.

The floor show started soon after they were seated, for which Alyson was thankful. It was taking a strenuous effort to overcome her bemused state. What had come over her? she wondered, casting surreptitious glances at the attractive profile of the man seated across from her. His attention was focused on the spotlighted singer crooning over a lost love, so she felt free to examine him without fear of being observed.

Relaxed in the half-light, Ivan looked more like an aristocratic Russian than the image of the aggressive Greek he usually projected. How would his dark, relatively short-cropped hair feel under her fingers? she wondered. Would it be coarse and springy or silky soft? And his clearly defined lips, sensuous now that he was relaxed—would they be harshly demanding or gently questing on her mouth? The curling sensations building deep within her warned of what her imagination was doing to her, and of the danger of those thoughts.

Her mouth became dry and she reached for her cocktail. The movement brought Ivan's attention to her. Lights glittered deep in his eyes, alerting her that he was sensitive to her every movement.

The whole thing was silly, Alyson chastised herself, and she turned her attention to the singer. She had enough men friends without being lured by one of Ivan's caliber. With this Greek, her intuition warned her, any relationship could plunge her into a whirlpool of unplumbed emotions. Already he had made her nerves vibrate with an unaccustomed awareness that held a tinge of apprehension.

Ivan Kyriokos was not for her, she decided firmly. He had made his first play, and it was up to her to call a halt to any further advances. She wasn't interested in a man who showed contempt for women. What was it in his past that made him so callous?

A chilling resentment surfaced when she admitted to herself that he was probably thinking of her along the same lines. She shot him a hard look, which he happened to catch. His brow arched in surprise, but she refocused her attention on the flamenco dancers who now held the spotlight on the stage.

As soon as the floor show was over, Alyson decided it was definitely time to leave. Once out of his sight, he'd forget she was alive unless she was mentioned in reports that reached him from Ecuador. As far as she was concerned, that would be more than enough.

"Thank you for a very delightful evening," she said firmly. "We still have over an hour's drive ahead of us and we should leave." Bob got to his feet and helped her into her jacket while Ivan signaled for the bill. They were soon in the car and heading back to his place.

When parting at the parking lot, Alyson tolerated his hand as it slid one last time along her arm. He was simply enjoying the texture of the material, she told herself. And the caress in his eyes when they said their good-byes was only his male ego seeking a final response from her.

"You're quiet," Bob commented when he picked up Highway 95 North. He'd been discussing the coming trip and she'd remained suspiciously silent.

"Just tired," Alyson apologized. "It's been a long day for me." She shifted in her seat, irritated with herself. There was no reason for this depression. Ivan had been frank enough about the women in his life and their limited purpose.

In the busy rush of the following week, Alyson was able to relegate thoughts of their disturbing employer to the back of her mind. Since she had the luxury of adequate backing and a boat that could carry the supplies, she made certain that she'd be well stocked against eventualities.

Packing clothes for the two of them was easy. Weather permitting, they'd be living primarily in jeans or shorts and, of course, bathing suits. With time running out, Bob pressed her into service to help track down some of the backup gear needed in case there was a breakdown. Valves were known to get stuck and hoses could spring leaks, and masks that fit well one day were sometimes no longer snug the next. They'd worked closely before on such preparations, so the logistics didn't faze them. Alyson managed to borrow a van from a friend once it was apparent that their sports car couldn't transport the growing mound of supplies.

"Now I'm sorry that I'm not going with you," Alyson admitted when the day finally arrived for Bob to leave. They were packing the van, and her brother's jubilant anticipation of the imminent sailing was catching.

"You should have decided that before," he grumbled as he stacked packages of developing paper in one corner of the van. "I'm sure Elsa would like another woman along."

"Just remember, when you reach Panama, send a card with a picture of the canal," she told him. "Meanwhile I'll do my best to finish up this book. Did I tell you that the publisher called yesterday, urging me to get it to them?"

"It looks finished to me," Bob said, heaving gallon jugs of developing chemicals into place. "You really shouldn't have my name on the book, you know. Most of the photos are yours, and you're doing all the work in putting it together."

Alyson ignored his protest as he locked the back door of the filled van and frowned after checking his watch.

"We've got time for a shower and a quick lunch," she assured him. They were into November, but

Florida's summer weather was still holding, causing their T-shirts to cling damply to them from their exertions.

An hour later they were on the road, and another hour found them searching for the streets leading to the marina where the *Semele* was docked.

She was still a graceful boat, even with the heavy machinery bolted to her deck. Bill, looking more at ease in well-washed denims, came out of the wheel-house with a tall, stooped middle-aged man who was introduced as Tarry Smith, the engineer who was in charge of seeing that the pair of diesels got them to Ecuador.

Several dollies were commandeered and the van was quickly unloaded. After seeing to the stowing of the supplies, they wandered over the boat to check on the fittings.

They found Elsa in the cold-storage area, checking to see that the last of the frozen foods were correctly labeled before being placed in a huge freezer. She refused Alyson's offer of help with a smile. "This is one thing that I have to do myself so I know where everything is."

They moved on to meet the rest of the crew. Frank Doran emerged from under the table in the radio room, a soldering iron in his hand. He introduced himself as the radio operator.

"And navigator," Bill added, coming up behind them. "He swings a mean sextant. We'll be needing his expertise to put us accurately over the wreck." Though almost bald, Frank appeared to be their age. He had startling bushy red whiskers, and twinkling blue eyes that moved appreciatively over Alyson's slim figure.

"I knew I took this job for a reason." He grinned

cheekily. "I can already see moonlight nights on the deserted beach—"

"—dodging her brother, Bob," Bill cut in, winking at her.

The last one in the skeleton crew was another diver. Alyson had never met Jack Michaels but had heard of him. He had sun-bleached blond hair and almost white eyebrows and lashes, which contrasted strongly with his deep brown eyes. His smile was shy, and Alyson liked him immediately. From what she'd seen so far, Ivan had gathered a good working group together. Their stay in Ecuador should prove productive as well as enjoyable.

Elsa called them to the dining salon and announced she'd finished her job and had started a pot of coffee. Alyson was again swept with a wishful longing to join them as the talk centered enthusiastically on the imminent trip. No one had worked the Pacific coast of South America before, and, like Bob, all were eager for the new adventure.

Frank brought the charts covering the area of their exploration from the radio room and spread them on the table. They leaned over them, eager to examine them closer.

Bill, who was facing the door, stiffened and slowly came to attention. "Good afternoon, Mr. Kyriokos," he said respectfully. "I wasn't expecting you today or I'd have been outside to greet you."

All except Alyson turned in surprise. She was incapable of moving as she fought to control the heavy thudding of her heart. Her reaction appalled her. Fool that she was, she thought that he'd been successfully expelled from her mind for the past week. Yet, now, even before looking at him, her body was vibrating to a new beat.

"There's no need for that, Captain," Ivan said easily. "I came to check if you had success in finding the cause of the distortion on the radar screen."

"That's all fixed, sir," Frank said quickly. "It was a case of running down all the wires until I found a faulty connection."

"Good. And has all the food arrived as ordered?" he asked Elsa.

"Delivered and put away," she replied with satisfaction.

He questioned the engineer next. "And I assume everything is under control in your quarters, Smith?"

"The tanks have been topped and all's in working order, sir," Tarry returned promptly.

"Everything that we brought along has been stowed below," Bob answered Ivan's unasked question when the latter's gaze focused on him.

"And you've settled in?" Ivan asked Jack. He received a shy smile and a nod in the affirmative from the last crew member.

While talking, Ivan had been moving across the salon to where they sat around the table. He was devastatingly male in pale blue denim slacks and bush jacket. The top buttons to his shirt were open, baring his strong column of throat to Alyson's hungry gaze. She'd been impressed by him in his elegant tailored suits, but seeing him in this casual outfit made him seem more approachable and, as a result, raised havoc with her senses.

"I take it your equipment is also on board, Alyson?" He leaned over her shoulder while speaking, his attention caught by the chart spread before them.

"Yes, sir," she said in a strangled voice. His hand had moved across her back and his fingers found the small opening where her blouse was buttoned at the back of her neck. A lick of fire touched her, and her cup clattered as she hurriedly placed it on the saucer.

The rat knew what he was doing to her, she fumed impotently as he took the seat beside her after agreeing to Elsa's offer of a cup of coffee.

Ivan's long, slender finger moved over the chart as he spoke on points of reference that they could use when at sea. He was no silent, behind-the-scenes "angel." He had at his fingertips every pertinent factor in the venture, and Alyson was certain it would be the same with anything he did. Would it be the same with people he was interested in? She recalled the file he had on them, and a chilled finger touched her spine. Just how thoroughly had he researched them before deciding that they were satisfactory? It was an unpleasant sensation that he could be privy to intimate information about her.

Elsa refilled everyone's cup before opening a box of cookies and spreading them on a platter. "Everything is on schedule," Bill announced with satisfaction as he palmed a handful of the sweets. "We'll be leaving at noon tomorrow. Will you be here to see us off?"

Ivan nodded in response. "I told my secretary to keep the time free." His gaze slid to the quiet woman beside him. "Are you planning to stay over?"

"I hadn't intended to," Alyson admitted. "But it would be fun. The trouble is, I might be tempted to sneak on board. Would you make me swim back if you caught me stowing away?" she asked Bill with a grin.

"Never," he replied, an answering smile on his lips. "I'd keep you chained, though, and have you swab the decks as punishment."

"You're a cruel man." she sighed with exaggerated regret. It would have been fun to make the trip with them, she admitted again with a pang of regret.

She helped Elsa clean up before returning to say her good-byes. It had grown later than she realized. With the sun setting earlier, she'd be driving home in the dark if she didn't hurry.

"I meant to take you out to dinner," Bob said when she found him. He was bending over a compressor pump with Jack, the other diver. They had wrenches in their hands and several parts were lying on the floor beside them. "I decided to test this and found it overheating. Some jerk put a section in backwards. We have to check that it hasn't caused any stress on the motor. It's only the backup pump, but it might be in critical demand at some point."

It could well happen, Alyson knew. "I didn't notice how late it is. If I leave now, I'll be hitting all the evening traffic. I think it would be smarter to eat here and leave after the rush is over. Do you know a good Cuban restaurant close by, Jack?"

Her first thought had been to return to the Greek restaurant where Ivan had taken them, but she wasn't dressed appropriately. By now she felt a little worse for wear in her jaunty red-and-white striped knit top and designer jeans.

"I'll be happy to take you to one I know," Ivan said, coming up silently behind her.

Oh, no you don't! was her first instinctive reaction, but his expression was bland, even somewhat indifferent, so that she felt foolish. After that one tingling touch on her back, he had practically ignored her, and she was left to wonder if it could have been an accident. The touch had been brief enough, and he could have been bracing himself when he bent over the chart. Even now his attention was focused on the problem the men were trying to resolve, as if unconcerned about her answer.

"Let me know tomorrow if you were able to fix it," he ordered. "If not, I'll have a replacement sent down."

He turned to her and asked briskly. "Ready to leave? I know that everyone must have a hundred last-minute details to attend to, so we'll let them get on with them."

His fingers touched her elbow, urging her to the boarding plank. It would be childish to refuse his invitation, she reasoned, despite the faint warnings in her mind, trying to be heard. Besides, she loved ethnic food, and he'd already shown that he knew the best places. "Where shall I meet you?" she asked, stopping by her van.

He glanced at the thin gold watch on his wrist. "It's still a little early to eat, and I have a few telephone calls I must make. Follow me to my place and you can leave the van there. We'll use my car."

She should have known. Was it pay now, feeding time later?

Sensing her rebellion, Ivan's dark eyes snapped. "For heaven's sake," he said with growing irritation. "It's been a long day for me and I'm hungry. A seduction scene is the last thing that I'm contemplating."

If he'd been mocking or sardonic, or brought his considerable sensuality into play, Alyson would have refused him. But he was the businessman, trying not to show his annoyance over the delay. She unlocked the van without another word and waited until he had backed out the Lincoln before following him to the underground parking lot beneath his condo.

His houseman met him at the door, and after a short exchange in Greek he handed Ivan a sheet of paper.

"Giorgio will show you where you can freshen up. Tell him what you want to drink," he said while scanning the list in his hand. "My secretary advises that I make these calls. I'd better get them done so we can enjoy the rest of the evening."

He strode to his study after an absentminded "Excuse me," and Alyson was led down the hallway to a guest room. Giorgio hurriedly checked to see that the bathroom was outfitted with clean towels before he asked what she wished to drink. "No need to hurry, Miss O'Hare," he advised from experience. "Those telephone calls always seem to take more time than he anticipates."

Alyson hid her amusement and murmured her understanding. His voice held just the correct amount of regret, as if he knew how Ivan must feel about being denied her company. The nuance could only have come from long practice.

The bathroom was in white marble, to which Ivan seemed partial. It was edged in black onyx decorated with the Greek *Meandros* design in gold. The fixtures were gold, and the result was truly elegant.

She quickly combed her hair and washed her face before applying a light touch of makeup. Leaving the bedroom, she noticed that the furniture was from the Queen Anne period. She knew that they were original pieces.

"It's still warm on the balcony," Giorgio hinted when handing her a Campari and soda.

Alyson smiled her approval. She hoped that Ivan appreciated Giorgio's superlative memory. He even recalled her delight over the view.

Evening had descended, and except for a scattering of pinpoints of light that told of night fishermen, the ocean was a dark expanse. Yet, even this high up she was aware of the pulsing movement of the vast body of water as the swells rose and fell in a timeless and constant undulation. I am infinity, it seemed to say. What matters your minute allotment of time? Alyson drew away with a small shiver, unwilling to indulge in morbid introspection.

"Is it too chilly, Miss O'Hare?" Giorgio asked solicitously. He placed a small chafing dish on the table next to a lounge chair and lit the Sterno underneath it to keep the contents hot.

"Not at all," she assured him, sniffing appreciatively when he raised the lid and a heavenly aroma reached her. She selected one of the skewered cabbage-wrapped sausages. "I could make a meal of these alone," she sighed in delight after biting into it.

"They are a favorite of Mr. Kyriokos," Giorgio confided before leaving.

Alyson relaxed on the lounge chair and slowly ate the tasty concoctions. Ivan be damned, she muttered petulantly. She was hungry, and if he spent much more time on the phone, he'd just have to forfeit his share!

Giorgio brought her a fresh Campari and a feather-light cashmere cover, which he draped solicitously across her legs. She was surprised to see that an hour had passed. While sipping the drink, she wondered if it was wise to stay any longer. Ivan was involved with the problems inherent in keeping his private empire under control and had no doubt forgotten about her. It made sense to leave, she told with herself while reaching for another of Giorgio's delicious offerings. Settling deeper into the soft cushions, the decision was reached that she'd leave as soon as she finished her drink.

She drifted into a dreamy half-sleep. The past three days had been hectic. She and her brother had gone to bed late the night before after finishing a last check to see that they'd obtained everything on the lists.

"My apologies." A slender finger slid along her cheek, causing Alyson to raise sleep-heavy eyes. "The connection with Japan was poor, and it took much longer than I expected to wind up my business."

A vagrant breeze caused the Sterno to flicker. Ivan raised the lid on the chafing dish and took one of the two remaining morsels. "At least Giorgio saw to it that you didn't starve," he said, popping one in his mouth. "It gets cool out here once the sun goes down."

"The blanket kept me comfortable," she replied. Resenting his nonchalance, she reached for the last hors d'oeuvre as a small gesture of retaliation. A glance at her wristwatch brought her out of the chair. "I didn't know it was this late!" she exclaimed. How could she have wasted almost three hours waiting for him!

"It's almost ten. Most places are closed by now!" she accused testily. "The only reason I decided to have dinner here was because I didn't want to get caught in the commuter rush. I'll leave now—the highways should be less congested."

Long fingers closed around the tender skin of her upper arm. He turned her to the living room and closed the glass door against the damp night. "It is late by American standards," he admitted. "However, I'm used to eating at this time. I told Giorgio to prepare a meal for us. It shouldn't take long." He released his hold to go to the bar and mix himself a drink. "Would you like another?" he asked, raising a dark eyebrow as his gaze slid over her, making her realize how disheveled she must look.

Immediately on guard, Alyson shook her head. She'd had two drinks more than he, and on a comparatively empty stomach, so she considered it wise to refrain from tempting fate with a third. A meal in his apartment was a far cry from sharing one in a restaurant.

She glanced warily at him and noticed for the first time the weariness shadowing his eyes. It gave her an inkling of the tremendous pressure he must work under, and an appreciation of how he must need this quiet time to relax.

As Ivan promised, their wait was short. Alyson marveled again at Giorgio's culinary skill. The first course was *soupa avgolemeno*, a lemon soup garnished with chopped dill. She barely restrained herself from a second helping of the chicken pilaf, tender morsels on a bed of brown rice and onions, and garnished with almond slivers and raisins. The mixed green salad had cubed feta—the slightly sour goat cheese—and Greek olives, for which she'd developed a passion when in that country. Like Ivan, she decided against a sweet dessert. Upon his urging she sampled the large array of cheeses that Giorgio offered.

"I hope the meal was an acceptable substitute for the one you desired," Ivan said when they settled on the curved sofa in the living room, where they were served the Greek coffee. "Giorgio wouldn't hear of it when I suggested he cook a Cuban meal."

She smiled at the imperturbable servant as he adjusted the coffee pot so that it would be easy for her to serve seconds. "That was only because I didn't know I'd have the good fortune to enjoy one of his superb meals again."

The flowers this time, Alyson noticed, were the lovely huge Transvaal daisies in the full range of their heavenly colors, from yellow through all the peach tones and to deep rose. Did he change the color accent each week? she wondered. If so, using flowers was a novel way to accomplish it.

While all the lamps were lit, the rheostat that controlled their brilliance was adjusted so that the room was bathed in a soft glow. Alyson's glance slid over Ivan after she refilled his cup. He'd made no pass at her; in fact their conversation had been rather decorous. Still, she couldn't help being sensitive to the vibrations that were passing between them, making her skin prickle with awareness. Was it simply her reaction to the overwhelming masculinity of the man? Could it be possible that he was unconscious of the sensual aura he exuded even when he was relaxed? The thought made her sip cautiously at the steaming black coffee.

"Was your mother's name Semele?" she was startled to hear herself ask. He impaled her with a harsh look. "I . . . I was wondering because of the name of your boat," she stammered, disconcerted by his forbidding expression.

Good heavens, could it be named after his wife? Did he have one tucked away in his villa in Greece, a complacent woman content to remain behind, perhaps raising his children? The idea shook her.

His gaze was watchful over the rim of his cup. "Her name was Anastasia," he replied slowly.

"I heard that she was Russian," Alyson admitted over her bewilderment. Why was he acting as if he were testing her? "I was fascinated by the unusual name, so I looked it up in one of my books on mythology," she continued when he made no further comment. She shifted in her seat, wishing uncomfortably that she'd never brought up the subject.

He finished his coffee before replying. "Then you know Semele had a son named Dionysus."

"Yes, the story intrigued me." Mainly because Dionysus was Ivan's middle name. She wanted to question him further but held back. Something was definitely bothering him. She hoped he wasn't thinking that she was prying into his private life.

His curled lashes lowered, veiling his black eyes before he answered. "According to legend, she was tricked into asking Zeus to expose himself in the full splendor of his divinity. She didn't know that as a mortal she'd be burned to ashes if she ever saw him that way."

A shiver touched her. "The old gods were certainly quick with their revenge!" she murmured while watching the smooth way he moved when he leaned forward to place his empty cup on the low table before them.

"It was a private name my father had for my mother, and came about from the way they met. They happened to be on a cruise ship at the same time and there was a flash fire. My father heard a woman's scream from one of the cabins and he dashed through the wall of flame to rescue her. Later my mother insisted that that was how she first saw him, encased in fire. Luckily, other than having his hair singed, he was unhurt."

His mouth twisted in an ironic smile. "One of his middle names was Zeus. When she teased him about it, he retaliated by calling her Semele."

"How lovely!" Alyson sighed, caught by the romantic overtones. "Of course, their son had to be called Dionysus! No other name would have been fitting."

"You may think so," Ivan said wryly. "But I remember my first bloody nose, at the tender age of six, was the result of a schoolmate teasing me about it."

She looked at him in surprise. "But when we were in Skyros, I had the definite impression that your countrymen still hold their old gods in respect."

He gave a negligible shrug. "At that age I resented their accusations that I was acting as if I were a god. I had to show them that I was a mere mortal just as they were."

Her smile was tender as she invisioned a small boy with black curly hair defying his peers, not understanding at that young age that he already carried himself with an air that set him apart.

"It got worse when I went to the university in England and they realized that Dionysus was the Greek counterpart of the Roman Bacchus."

Laughter lit up her eyes. "I daresay part of it was because you lived up to that name," she teased.

His eyes frosted before melting under her impudent grin. "It wasn't that bad," he said with a shake of his head.

It amazed Alyson how that small exchange lightened the rest of the conversation. When young, had he really resented the attitude he encountered because of his name?

"The search boat was my father's yacht," Ivan explained, finally answering her original question. "He naturally christened it with his special name for my mother. Unfortunately I can find little time to use it, and it's become too costly to maintain. When I became interested in this venture, I decided to have it converted. My mother would have understood," he added in a low voice, as if an afterthought. "She was interested in history and was

66

always sponsoring some dig or underwater exploration."

"We'll have to celebrate their send-off tomorrow in her memory with a glass of champagne," Alyson murmured, captured by this new gentle part of him that she didn't know existed.

His brow rose. "Then you plan to be there tomorrow?"

"I wouldn't miss it," she promised. Glancing at her watch, she gave a small gasp upon noting the time. "It's almost midnight!" she cried in surprise.

"It doesn't make much sense to drive home, only to have to turn around and return," he protested. "Wouldn't it be wiser to stay over?"

"It would if I had a change of clothes with me," Alyson replied, barely hiding an escaping yawn. She was suddenly very tired and admittedly dreaded the almost two-hour drive ahead of her before she'd be home in bed. "I don't even have a toothbrush, though I guess I could buy one someplace."

"I'm sure Giorgio can find one for you. And from what I know about women's personal clothes, yours should dry overnight on the heated bar in the bathroom."

Her eye flew to Ivan's and, realizing what he was offering, she was immediately on guard.

"You look like a cornered virgin," he mocked her. "Don't tell me you're not sophisticated enough to accept an invitation to spend a night in a man's *guest room!*"

Alyson studied his bland expression, wondering why she felt as if he'd deliberately thrown down a gauntlet in challenge. Should she pick it up—or run?

"I've never forced myself on a woman, if that's what is bothering you, Alyson," Ivan added persuasively.

"I imagine you've never had to," she said dryly.

"So!" he said, rising before her and taking her hand to assist her from the comfortable nest she'd found in the pillows. "Let us alert Giorgio to see what he can provide."

How like him to assume she was bending to his will, she groused, astounded to find herself more amused than irritated. Still, reason dictated that his offer was a logical solution if she wanted to avoid the tiring trek home and back again.

Short minutes later Alyson found herself gazing around the bedroom, bemused by Ivan's adroit handling of the situation. A toothbrush and a tube of toothpaste had been produced by the unflappable Giorgio. No doubt experience had taught him to keep a supply on hand, she thought wryly.

Alyson adjusted a large towel around herself when she returned from her shower. She found the bedspread removed and the pink satin sheet turned neatly back on the queen-size bed. Draped at the bottom was a fine lawn shirt, undoubtedly offered by the servant to use as a nightgown. It was evidently one of Ivan's. After several seconds of indecision, she slid her arms into the long sleeves and caught her breath as the soft material enclosed her like a caress.

There was no reason for her to experience the sensations that were running through her, she scolded herself. Every nerve ending quivered in a startling yet exquisite awareness when it struck her that the shirt had been in contact with Ivan's body, that the expensive silky-soft material ever slithered over him in precisely the same way. That thought sent her hurrying to the vanity to brush her hair with hard determined strokes that had her wincing.

Whoa, Alyson, she warned herself. Don't walk blindly into something you'll find it difficult to retreat from!

Her reflection in the gilt mirror over the dresser revealed how the thin material hid few of her curves. The shirttails barely reached her thighs, exposing her long golden legs in all their splendor. She turned back the sleeves. The provocative image struck her as humorous and she grinned, trying to picture what the effect would be on the all-too-sensuous man in the adjacent bedroom if he should see her in his shirt.

Alyson was tired but too restless to sleep. She berated herself for foolishly drinking all those cups of strong black coffee. Ivan might be used to indulging himself so late at night, but her body felt as if it were on a caffeine high. She paced the room, giving it the admiring attention it deserved. She hadn't seen Ivan's bedroom, but the rest of the rooms, while elegant, were rescued from being too austere by the lavish use of flowers and greenery. This guest room was more feminine, and she wondered who were the most frequent occupants, relatives or a parade of pillow friends.

The floor was covered with a plush white carpet. The graceful furniture was edged with gold. She had to laugh upon examining the enameled headboard of the wide bed and discovering it was painted with fat cupids and entwined roses and ivy. Had it served it's purpose in putting the occupants in the right mood?

Her laugh faded when she pictured a tall, rapier-lean man in the bed, a woman's fingers roughing the curls on his head into unaccustomed disarray. The fact that the woman had auburn hair and her sea-green eyes were drowsy with desire made Alyson turn abruptly from the bed to continue her examination of the room.

The walls were covered in a pale pink flocked cloth, and she drew a finger over the velvety composition to immediately recall how seductive fingers had slid over the dress she'd worn the last time, and Ivan's evident pleasure in the velvety suedelike material. He had proven innumerable times that he was a tactile person.

Enough! she upbraided herself, and went determinedly to the bathroom to see if there were any aspirin, which might help counteract her tenseness and permit her to sleep. She found some, and after swallowing two, her interest was caught by an array of perfume bottles. When she finished sniffing appreciatively at the assortment, she touched her pulse points with one that reminded her of a long-forgotten dew-laden rose garden that she'd once walked through early one morning. She'd at least match the roses entwined so beguilingly on the headboard of her bed!

Alyson was about to climb into the bed when the click of the door closing behind her alerted her that she was no longer alone. She whirled around in alarm to meet brooding black eyes.

"What are you doing here?" she cried after taking a deep breath to counteract the leap to her heart.

The white toweling of Ivan's robe ended at his knees, and she was certain that he had on nothing underneath. The derisive lift to his eyebrow was answer enough. There could be no doubt as to why he was in her bedroom.

Ivan's smile was mocking. "I came to see if you had everything you need for the night."

"Everything's fine," Alyson insisted hurriedly. It was taking a major effort to keep her hands by her side and not use them to cover herself. He'd be even more sardonic over that virginal display. His glance had already swept over her, and she knew the thin material had been an ineffectual screen from his knowledgeable eyes.

"I'm happy to see you're not offended by Giorgio's sense of propriety. He felt you should have a nightgown of some sort—at least a pajama top—but since I don't use pajamas, I didn't have one to offer." His velvet eyes stroked her with visible appreciation. "I must remember to commend him on his choice of garments."

"Well . . . ah . . . good night, Ivan. It's getting quite late." Was that thin, strained voice hers?

His smile became indolent as he took several long, measured strides toward her. He looked alarmingly like a predator, and she backed away instinctively until the backs of her knees pressed against the mattress and she could move no farther.

"No," she whispered, her head shaking to give the emphasis her voice seemed to lack. "You promised . . . you said you wouldn't . . ."

His brow rose in a disbelieving arch. "Are you intimating that you didn't expect me to come?" he asked in amazement.

Anger surfaced, giving her back her voice. "Of course!" she cried sharply, pulling herself so that he wouldn't loom over her so. She wasn't about to be intimidated. If he thought she was going to become another on his list of pillow friends, he had another thing coming!

"What do you think happens when you agree to stay overnight in a man's apartment?" he asked tauntingly.

"Very definitely not what you evidently believe!" she snapped. "If I happened to have acted the innocent in accepting your invitation, please excuse me for being so dense. If you'll go now, I'll get dressed and rectify your impression by leaving."

He made no attempt to step aside to give her room. She was forced to brush against him as she started stormily to where her clothes were draped over a chair.

His hand snaked out to grasp her shoulder to pull her abruptly against him. "Are you denying the attraction that's between us?" he asked throatily.

Dear Lord! she groaned to herself. The action had parted his robe so that his naked chest was pressed against her. She, too, could have been naked for all the protection her inadequate covering offered from the heat scorching her.

"You said that you never forced a woman," she said in a stricken voice that failed miserably to convey the cold rejection that she had intended. Her blood roared in her ears, making her light-headed.

"You are right. I've never had the need," he purred with assurance, and she wished her arms, suddenly treacherously weak, had the strength to push him away. Seeming to sense the quandary she was in, a small smile of masculine victory softened his lips before he fastened them to hers.

Alyson had enjoyed her share of kisses, but never had one so quickly activated her full response. When the tip of his tongue signaled his intention to explore further, her mouth opened readily for his full invasion, and she reveled in the quivers of delight that swept through her. When he finally raised his head, she was a torch burning with an all-consuming flame that only he could extinguish. She was only dazedly aware of how her body was pressed against his. His touch was necessary to ease her torment.

"Ivan," she whispered. Her hands moved from the muscles of his shoulders and crept up to brush the silken curls covering his head. How she'd longed to do this! She moaned while pulling his life-giving mouth back to hers in a thirsting, starving need for him to continue feeding the flames he had ignited.

"Yes, *agape mou,* I know," he answered huskily before reinvading the territory he'd already explored.

She was pressed back on the satin sheets and long fingers smoothly unfastened her shirt buttons. Her hands became thrillingly aware that he'd already discarded his robe, and his sinewy body pressed against hers once more. His were not the bulging muscles she was used to seeing, but hinted at the tensile agility of the fencing foil.

He brushed aside the fine cotton material of her shirt and moved his hand over her breast as if in epicurean evaluation, testing its weight before enjoying its fullness. Exquisite darts of flame shot inward, causing her body to arch, facilitating his exploration. They ached under his stroking, and the tips budded into a hard extension under his mind-wrecking massage.

He gave an impatient sound as he half raised her to remove the shirt. "My women soon learn not to bother with these trappings," he said huskily.

Alyson inhaled sharply as if suddenly doused with cold water. His women! The words rang like a loud warning. What a fool she was to have forgotten that she was obviously just one of many to him.

Because Ivan wasn't expecting it, she was able to

roll to the other side of the bed. She scrambled to her feet, her hands searching frantically for the open edges of the shirt to clutch them together.

"What—?" he began in surprise.

"I have no intention of being 'one of your women'!" Her cry was shrill.

Ivan rose to stand at the other side of the bed. He was naked, and his anger hadn't as yet counteracted his desire. Dear Lord! She quailed inwardly. Have him put something on! While her mind had regained control, her body was still screaming with frustration.

"What are you talking about?" he ground out forcefully.

"I'm telling you that I've no intention of becoming another notch in your bedpost," she returned icily. "I don't indulge in casual dalliances just because someone of the opposite sex happens to be available."

He looked at her disdainfully over his aristocratic nose. "And you believe that I do?"

For a moment Alyson felt fear upon seeing the anger burning in his eyes, and wondered if she'd gone too far; but she faced him bravely.

He shrugged on his discarded robe. "You, Miss Alyson O'Hare, have a lot to learn about me. I don't play games. Let us face facts: Ever since we met I never held a doubt that we'd end up as lovers. When you admit to and accept that irrefutable fact also, we'll proceed from there."

He snatched up his robe and belted it with a tug, his expression stern. "I'll leave now and give you time to come to terms with the inevitable."

His eyes slid appraisingly over her inadequately concealed body, resting with full appreciation on the curves enticingly delineated. The door closed firmly behind him. Alyson stared shakily at the white paneling. He had brought her emotions to a feverish pitch. The resulting turmoil raging within her was a warning she'd be wise to learn from. She drew in an uneven breath. She'd tasted his kisses. Would she be able to resist their lure? She closed her eyes, wishing desperately that she could refute his words.

5

Alyson sat on the side of the bed for long, tense minutes, staring at the closed door. She wouldn't put it past Ivan to return to stake his claim. Anyone with his expertise must know that she was left suffering under the crosscurrents of conflicting emotions, and that by this time regret would be uppermost over letting him go.

She knew if he came now, the war would be over. There wouldn't even be a preliminary skirmish. Her pulsating, swollen lips reminded her of the complete invasion they'd been subjected to. The inner ache had evolved into a painful longing laced with intense regret. Considering the turmoil he had caused, she marveled that she'd found the strength to reject him. He would be a superlative lover, she was certain, and she wondered traitorously if she'd been foolish to back away from the experience.

But what then? a voice warned. She didn't believe

in brief encounters. Would she be satisfied to be a name tacked on his list after Sharon's? Shuddering away from the thought, she crawled under the satin sheet. Surprisingly her healthy but tired body won, and she fell into an immediate sleep.

The next morning when she left her room for breakfast she was in full control of her emotions. With the bright sunshine lighting her room, it was easy to dismiss the events of the previous evening as the result of a normal chemistry between two attracted adults.

Ivan rose politely as she sat at the table set on the balcony. Just as politely he asked to be excused while he went through the letters piled by his plate.

"I wasn't able to attend to these last night. Since I'll be away again this morning, I won't have time to go over them with Sylvos," he explained, and immediately blanked out her presence.

She'd observed before his disconcerting ability to eliminate distractions when concentrating on what he considered to be more important. No doubt this was what made him so prosperous in his business, but Alyson was piqued. While dressing, she'd gone over different attitudes to take this morning when confronting him. It had never occurred to her that she'd be the one who would be ignored.

But it was too lovely a day to remain annoyed. The sun promised another warm afternoon, and the ocean moved in a calm swell that indicated that the *Semele*'s crew would have a smooth beginning to their trip.

Giorgio placed a dish of fresh fruit before her and she concentrated on enjoying the distinctive flavor of the papaya and mango slices. Bacon and eggs followed with light-as-a-feather popovers. The coffee was an American blend, and she had three cups before Ivan was through making his notations on the letters.

He leaned back in the chair, his long finger flicking a signal. Giorgio filled his cup before gathering the papers to take to the study. "Thank you for being patient and letting me finish what had to be done," he murmured while stirring the coffee.

Alyson pulled her attention from the freighter she'd been following as it sailed the edge of the Gulf Stream on it's way south, and looked at him in surprise. Did he actually think she'd have dared interrupt his intense concentration?

"You'll find that I'm never in the mood for inane gossip, and I tolerate it even less in the morning. It seems to be something most women like to indulge in."

Alyson's lashes hid her mocking gaze. "It makes me wonder what type of woman you're in the habit of sharing breakfast with," she replied. Her face was averted, so she was surprised to hear the low chuckle.

"Ah, *agape mou* has claws that like to draw blood! Although it's flattering, I wonder why you assume I'm such a womanizer."

"Oh, come now!" she muttered frostily. He was evidently enjoying himself and she refused to indulge his ego.

Flipping open a silver box that Giorgio had placed by his side, Ivan selected a thin cheroot. When it was lit, he leaned back in his chair and looked at her assessingly through the fragrant cloud of smoke. "The sad fact is that building a business, even one as modest as mine, leaves little time to waste pursuing the opposite sex."

"You wouldn't have to. They'd come to you," she retorted, never doubting her assertion. "You're handsome enough, and your wealth is undoubtedly an added attraction that few women can ignore."

Muscles knotted along his lean jaw. "But not with you." The question was barely concealed.

"Never me," she affirmed. His wealth would be a hindrance as far as she was concerned.

"But last night you would have been mine if I had insisted."

Alyson had wondered if he'd make any reference to the explosion of emotions that had erupted between them. "You did play the heavy seduction bit," she admitted carelessly, as if she'd survived better attempts.

He leaned forward, bringing his face close to hers. "If I recall correctly, you were an active participant."

For one heart-stopping moment she thought he was going to kiss her. Unconsciously her lids drooped heavily and her lips softened in anticipation. He drew back, and she fought the urge to slap away the smile of satisfaction he displayed. Darn him! He'd been toying with her, letting her know he wasn't fooled by her act.

"I admit this conversation with you has certain elements I'd like to pursue," he said agreeably. "However, if we want to catch the *Semele* before it departs, we'd better leave at once."

When they descended to the underground parking area, Ivan stopped by her van. "It would be best if you take it," he advised. "In order to fit in this send-off, my afternoon schedule has become crowded, and I won't have time to drive you back. Follow me. I know a shortcut to the marina."

The parting of the ways had begun. On more than one occasion Alyson had thought that their meeting would be the last one. Now she wondered if this would be it after they waved the boat off. So much for his assertion last night that they'd become lovers! she berated herself, aware of a regret reverberating in a hollow void growing within her. It took a concentrated effort for her to follow the Lincoln. It had been her decision to halt his seduction, so she'd better come to terms with the sense of loss.

They found everybody on board the ship was busy with last-minute activities. Final deliveries were being stowed as the countdown began. When boarding, Ivan had handed Elsa several bottles of champagne to chill. He now opened them and toasts were made to the success of the costly venture.

Bob had been happily surprised to see her, and she was angry with herself for letting him assume that she'd stayed at a motel. She could imagine his reaction if he knew about her stay in Ivan's apartment, and consoled herself by remembering that Bob seemed to have forgotten about Ivan's ulterior motive where she was concerned.

Don't be obtuse, Alyson upbraided herself. From that first encounter there'd been a special electric charge between them. It would have been impossible to hide it from any observer, and Bob hadn't been blind. She caught her breath, hearing again Ivan's assertion that it was inevitable that they would be lovers. Her body tingled with a new life, effectively mocking her heart, which was warning her she'd be a fool to succumb to his seductive words.

Fighting the conflicting emotions, she frowned unseeingly out the window. She wished she had never met Ivan.

"Why the frown, Alyson? Do you want to stay on board?"

"Don't you feel the urge to go along?" she challenged as she looked up at the tall Greek.

His lashes shadowed his eyes while he searched her face, as if looking for something. "Are you missing your brother already? I can understand the special closeness between twins, but don't you think it's time to consider cutting that tie? You can't always mother him. He can never become a full man as long as he has you to lean on."

She gritted her teeth in resentment. She'd been getting too many of those innuendos lately. "In spite of what you think, we each have a very active life in which the other doesn't intrude. But thank you for your *fatherly* advice."

She had the perverse pleasure of seeing a dusky flush darken his cheeks. It was very satisfying to know that she could score against him.

Fingers clamped around the soft flesh of her arm. It was the only sign of his anger, and it was more awesome because of the control that kept his face expressionless. "Then I should have taken that 'active life' into consideration last night and not left you so soon."

There was a warning and something else that she couldn't read in his eyes that caused a tremor to run through her. He could be a dangerous man when crossed.

"Your hand, Mr. Kyriokos," she hissed. "Is it your intention to leave your imprint on my arm?"

He looked startled for a moment as if unaware of the pressure he was exerting. The tension was released, but not the hold. "You are becoming a very irritating young woman." A speculative look crossed his face. "I wonder if that is your intention. Are you trying to provoke me into making certain that my prediction about us comes true?"

She gave him a withering glance, too wise to

attempt an answer to that loaded question. "I think the captain is anxious to leave. If you'll excuse me, I'd like to say my final good-byes."

With commendable dignity Alyson descended the gangplank to where Bob was loosening the last of the dock lines. He tossed them to Jack, who was coiling them on the deck.

"Have a safe trip," she said, placing a farewell kiss on his cheek. "I'll see you in Ecuador in two weeks."

He pulled her to his broad chest in a bear hug. "For heaven's sake, take care," he admonished gruffly, his gaze on the tall, slender man approaching them. "I don't want you to get hurt."

Ivan gave no indication if he heard or caught the warning look aimed at him. "Smooth sailing, Bob," he said, offering his hand. "I've sent word ahead to the Indian couple who are taking care of the villa that you'll be arriving shortly. Elsa will oversee the place once you arrive. Don't worry about your sister. I'll see that she gets there."

The last line was released and Bob leaped on board. The heavy throb of the diesels increased, and the space widened between the boat and dock. Alyson waved, but everyone was too busy with their various jobs for a last look to shore, and her hand dropped as a sense of loss invaded her.

It seemed as if this parting from her twin was more than just the distance the boat was putting between them. It was true that Bob and she were very close. Was Ivan right? Was their special closeness blocking the development of a deeper emotional involvement with a possible life partner? They were twenty-eight, and if she wished to start the family she dreamed of, it was time to think seriously about that possibility.

Alyson was always the better organizer of the two.

She recognized that her carefree brother could well be depending on her for the stability she offered, the stability that a wife should be supplying. A sigh escaped her as she reached the van. She unlocked the door and gave a start when Ivan's hand slid from behind her to pull it open.

"Are you leaving without saying a proper good-bye?" he asked. The mocking light he seemed to reserve for her had returned in his eyes.

"Of course not," Alyson denied hurriedly to hide her embarrassment. "I did thank Giorgio, but I should certainly thank my host, too." He'd given her a delightful meal and a comfortable bed to sleep in. If in the process he had also torn her life loose from its safe mooring with his kisses, that was her problem.

Alyson extended her hand, but Ivan ignored it. He placed a finger under her chin to angle her lips for his taking. It was a light, teasing kiss, one that left her unhappily hungering for more. When he withdrew, their eyes met, and he gazed long into the shimmering blue-green depths.

"*Epeph!*" he swore under his breath, and his mouth descended to take full possession of her offering with an unexpected urgency.

I shouldn't let this happen! Alyson moaned even as her lips parted for his invasion. What was it about his kisses that rendered her muscles, her bones, so useless that she melted against him as if seeking needed sustenance from his sinewy strength?

His fingers fanned over her throat. He had no hold on her; yet, as the kiss deepened, she was bound to him as if with bands of steel. This is madness, and in broad daylight! It was an incoherent cry immediately lost in the tidal wave of the emotions swamping her. How easily he could trigger them!

Slowly, reluctantly, Ivan retreated from his foray. Alyson was conscious of the unassuaged hunger in his eye fastened on her swollen mouth, and that the vein pulsing at his temple was throbbing with the same intensity as the one in her throat, on which one of his fingers rested.

His gaze observed the erratic rise and fall of her breasts before sliding to the slim gold watch on his wrist. "This is poor timing on our part, yes?" he murmured huskily. "We'll have to do better next time."

Ivan stepped back, and only then was she aware of the grinning faces of the nearby workers at the marina. One gave a thumbs-up sign of approval before Ivan stepped to block him from view.

"Get in," he ordered with a show of impatience as he held the door open for her. "I have to hurry or I'll be late for my appointment. Drive safely, Alyson. I'll be in touch."

Her head shook in a denial. She wanted to shout "No!" but her throat wouldn't function. She jabbed the key in the ignition, irritated over the way her hand trembled. Keeping her face averted, she sent the car wheels spinning as she raced out of the parking area. Her only thought was to place miles between them.

How could he kiss her like that and then in seconds act impatient over missing an appointment? She was taunted by the galling conviction that, of the two of them, she'd been the only one so affected, that it had been his expertise and not any deeper involvement on his part that had started her emotions on their wild rampage. Fool, fool, fool! The refrain was picked up by the spinning wheels and continued until she was safe in her driveway.

A long soak in a steaming bubble bath partially

soothed her frayed nerves and permitted her to view the encounter in a calmer manner. What in the world had caused her to react so strongly? She could admit honestly that he had meant the kiss to be only a casual farewell. It had changed character only after he'd seen the begging look in her eyes. She was the one who had hungered for more, and he had complied, as any other man would have done.

Alyson pulled the drain in the tub and stepped out to dry herself briskly with annoyance. Take care, her brother had warned. He didn't want her to get hurt.

Her face was drawn as she reached for clean underwear. She had a disconcerting sensation that his warning had come too late.

6

Alyson watched with a feeling of accomplishment as the postmaster attached the stamps to the boxed manuscript. She'd spent every waking minute of the past week finishing it. There'd be some editorial polishing before it finally went into print, but the hard part was over.

She walked out of the post office riding a high. The mental and emotional release after days of intense concentration always triggered this freedom from tension, resulting in elation. If only there were someone to celebrate with! At times like this she usually went on a double date with Bob, or they had a group of friends in. But her brother was on the Pacific by now, and she'd been so engrossed in finishing the book that she hadn't let her friends know that she was back in town.

She contemplated treating herself to a fancy restaurant, but eating a solitary meal surrounded by families or lovers didn't appeal to her. The result was that she stopped at the meat market and bought an outrageously expensive steak, soothing her conscience by telling herself that it would even out by supplying sandwich meat for several lunches. Passing the wine section, she added a bottle of rosé that she particularly liked. If she was going to celebrate, she might as well do it in style!

Still riding her high, it became a game. She lolled with sensuous delight in the tub of steaming water, the bath oil giving her skin the slickness of silk. The released scent called to mind moonlit nights with the air heavy from the heady perfume of night-blooming flowers.

The mood carried her on, leading her to select her sexiest garment. She would pretend she was dressing for a lover, that the meal she was preparing was for a party of two. It had been a long time since she had shared passionate kisses with Dimitri on that moon-drenched beach. Kisses with another, more virile Greek were carefully blanked from her mind. She was determined to play out her fantasy the way *she* wanted it to go.

She stepped into a shimmering jump suit. Grasping the tassled end of the zipper, she pulled it fully to the high neckline before pausing and tugging it down a few inches. What the heck, she grinned, a fun reck-lessness invading her. This was *her* night to playact the way she wished. The tassle was lowered to scant inches above her waist to expose tantalizing glimpses of the soft white mounds of her breasts.

The silken material was sinfully erotic against the bare flesh as well as to the eye. Without the obstruction of underwear, it molded her slender, full-breasted body in loving outline. Passion purple, Bob had called it when she'd worn it one evening. The whistles and slightly ribald comments from their guests had been pointed enough so that she had never had the courage to wear it again.

But tonight she could be as sexy as she wished, and since that was the mood she was riding, she decided to indulge herself. There was no reason she couldn't enjoy her solitary meal with a phantom lover if that was what pleased her, she decided with an indulgent laugh, and promptly sprayed a generous mist of her new perfume, letting it settle over her.

The table on the patio was carefully set with her best china, and to complete the atmosphere, she found and placed a long tapered candle in the center before pouring the chilled rosé into a crystal glass. As her brother would say, she was "putting on the dog," but didn't her phantom lover deserve the best?

She moved around the living room, loving the way the slick material slid over her skin, clinging, caressing with each movement. Sipping the wine, she immersed herself in her fantasy. "Monsieur X" would drive up soon and she'd float to the door, leaving a tantalizing trail of perfume that would soon captivate him. His dark, velvety eyes would envelope her with a hunger that told of his building desire as he handed her a florist's box in which sat one perfect green orchid.

"For you, my darling," he would say, letting a finger glide sensuously over her smooth cheek. "The petals remind me of the velvet texture of your skin; the green is for the color your eyes become when we make love." He'd enfold her in his arms, unable to fight his need to touch her, to inhale her scent, to indulge in the taste of her warm skin. Meanwhile her hand would fondle his close-cropped curly hair and their lips would meet. . . .

Alyson blinked as the bubble burst, dropping her out of her erotic fantasy. The doorbell was ringing. "Damn!" she muttered, "Just when the dream was getting good!" She had to laugh at herself as she went to answer the door. She hadn't indulged in fantasizing with such realism since she was a teenager.

She flicked on the front light before opening the door, and blinked again. Her phantom Monsieur X hadn't been given a name, but he had one now.

"Why, Ivan, hello!" she cried in surprise. He looked impossibly handsome in a gray silk suit that fit perfectly. The overhead bulb highlighted him against the growing dusk, accentuating the leashed power that was such an integral part of the man.

Ivan's eyes moved swiftly from the auburn hair haloed around Alyson's head, to pause momentarily on her slightly parted lips before gliding over her body, exquisitely sheathed in purple, and slowly back again. His breath caught when probing the plunging neckline and the exposed cleavage, then was released in a hiss from between his teeth. The sound vibrated like a tuning fork along Alyson's nerves, sending heat waves washing through her.

His smoldering eyes lost some of their fire when they shifted from the partially emptied glass of wine she was holding; he peered over her shoulder and around the living room. "I see that I should have called before dropping in on you like this." His voice was cool.

It was obvious that he thought she was entertaining and, after seeing her in the revealing jumpsuit, that the party was a very private one. She hid a smile and lowered her lashes so that the mischief glinting in her eyes wouldn't give her away.

"Do come in," Alyson murmured huskily, stepping

back to permit his entrance. "This is a pleasant surprise. What brought you this far north from Miami?"

"I had a business appointment in Stuart this afternoon and remembered when passing through Jupiter that you lived here. The meeting ended later than anticipated. I thought that I'd stop by, hoping you could recommend a good restaurant and that you would accompany me."

She waved him to a seat in the living room and had to swallow the laugh upon seeing his eyes dart questioningly to the kitchen and the doors leading to the bedrooms, obviously wondering in which room her lover was hiding and why.

"Would you like a drink?" Alyson asked demurely. "If you wish a mixed cocktail, though, you'll have to make it yourself. That's always been Bob's department. I've never learned the proportions."

"Thanks for the warning. A martini should never be left to the hands of an amateur." Ivan followed her to the kitchen divider, where she indicated the cabinet that held their store of liquor.

Leaning negligently against the counter after topping her wineglass, Alyson watched him mix a very dry martini. She was conscious of the teasing devil in her as part of her continuing high. That she had this self-assured man off-center pleased her no end. He'd been too irritatingly certain that he was the one in control of their encounters, and she grabbed happily at the idea that this opportunity presented a way to score a point on him.

While Ivan tasted his cocktail, she undulated down the short hall to her bedroom, knowing exactly how the glossy silk was moving over her firm derriere. She felt his eyes on her as she closed the door to her room before turning back to him, a secret smile on her lips. Sorry, Monsieur X, she laughed to herself, feeling deliciously wicked. You're locked in there for as long as I can keep him fooled!

She met Ivan's hard stare with wide, innocent eyes, which she lowered when his gaze went thoughtfully to the closed door. "I don't know about my going with you," she said softly, letting the reluctance linger in her voice. "But we have several very good restaurants that I can recommend to you. What type food are you interested in?" She returned with him to the living room, making certain he was receiving the full benefit of her new perfume, which was supposed to have remarkable effects on men.

"I was more interested in the charming company," Ivan admitted, waiting until she chose a wicker chair before sinking to the couch across from her.

Catching his puzzled expression, Alyson took a sip of wine to camouflage her smirk. He was too intelligent and would soon figure out her charade, but she intended to milk it as much as she could. She'd face his reaction when the time came, she decided with nonchalance. Meanwhile she was enjoying acting the siren too much to worry. She lowered the glass and ran the tip of her tongue along her lower lip to catch a clinging drop of wine before leaning back in the chair to stretch her long legs provocatively in front of her. A lone finger rubbed ever so slowly along her thigh, smoothing the silken material. She wished it was velvety, remembering his reaction to that texture.

She glanced at him in time to catch the way his nostrils flared, and she almost burst into laughter. This was *fun*. She had never before thought she could enjoy playing this type of game.

"Thank you, Ivan," she purred. "I really would

have loved to go with you, but you see . . ." Her voice trailed off as she raised her hands and let them flutter down in an apologetic regret. She never knew she could be such a consummate actress.

He rose up before her and she couldn't suppress a start, but he only raised his empty glass and moved to the kitchen. "I think I mixed enough for a second. Do you mind?"

"Of course not," she replied. "I'm allergic to gin and I'd have to throw it away."

He returned immediately with his filled glass and the wine bottle. "I thought you were low," he said, filling her glass before she could stop him.

Alyson suddenly remembered that breakfast had consisted of coffee and a single slice of toast. Her growling stomach and growing light-headedness alerted her to the fact that it had been a long time ago. She'd be wise to get some food in her—and soon. But how was she gracefully going to get him to leave?

Ivan placed the bottle and his glass on the coffee table and startled Alyson by taking off his jacket. He tossed it on a chair, and her eyes widened as he worked loose his necktie. It followed the jacket's flight to the chair.

"Wh-what are you doing?" she stammered, only then seeing the determined look on his face, and knew that fun-and-games time was over.

"I," he stated forcefully, "think it's time to take you up on what you've been offering. I've had enough of you wriggling that delightful tail at me, and if you'd like your thigh caressed, I'll be only to happy to oblige."

"No!" Her refusal was a squeak over the wild fluttering of her heartbeat.

"Yes," he returned as he calmly loosened the gold

cuff links on his shirt-sleeves before undoing the buttons down the front. Her pulse thickened as he bared his chest.

She stared in fascination at the light brush of hair across his chest. He took a step closer to her, appearing alarmingly tall, and she shrank into the seat cushions. There was no escape even if she tried to scoot awkwardly over the arms of the chair. But that wasn't her way. She'd had her fun, and if she had to pay the price, she'd go with all flags flying.

"There never was anyone else here," he accused darkly. "I just realized that when I saw your table on the patio set for only one person."

So that was what had tipped him off! "I never said there was," she countered sweetly. "You arrived at that assumption on your own." Laughter rose in her throat over his being fooled for so long, only but she suppressed it. Her lips quivered and she clamped even white teeth on them to hide the giveaway.

"Then who in the hell were you dressed for?" he demanded, his gaze sweeping scorchingly over her. "No woman wears something as tantalizing as that outfit just for her own entertainment!"

"Perhaps I was expecting you," she challenged daringly.

His chest expanded as he drew in a deep breath. This time the hiss through his teeth held a warning that caused a jangling along every nerve. "I'm glad to hear that." His voice was velvet-soft, matching his eyes. "It makes what happens next all the more pleasurable."

Danger! The bells clanged their warning. She'd better stop her foolishness at once or be prepared to pay for her folly. She stood up so he wouldn't loom so intimidatingly tall over her, only to realize at once that the move was a mistake. He was inches away from her, and the heat waves emanating from his body seemed to create a vacuum, sucking her close.

"This has gone far enough," she said, striving to sound and act calm and controlled while trying to deny her body's burning, crying for contact with his. Her head wanted to find the comfort of his shoulder so that her lips could taste the flesh along the strong column of his neck. Her arms ached to encircle his waist so that her soft curves could find the harsher angles of his male body. Instead she raised her chin with a defiant thrust.

"Today, after finally finishing my manuscript and sending it off, I felt like celebrating. Since there was no one available, I decided to do it by myself. I just happened to pick this outfit after taking my bath. Surely that's not a crime, is it?"

"The only crime is that all this loveliness might have gone to waste," he said. His accent thickened, a habit she'd noticed before when he was aroused. "I shall have to thank the gods for sending me here tonight and giving me the privilege of celebrating with you."

She cocked her head and laughed up at him. "Do you mean Zeus?" she teased.

A hand came up to run long, sensitive fingers over the silken covering on her arm. "More likely his son, Dionysus," he murmured suggestively, his mouth softening into a sensuous curve. "Remember, he was the one who had the women dancing around him in wild abandonment, eager to perform for his pleasure." The corners of his mouth deepened as he felt the tremor running through her.

She met his eyes and felt herself drowning in their dark depths, but knew she was helpless to save herself. His hand continued its slow progress across her shoulder and down, to rest a moment over her full breast. At that precise moment she knew she didn't want to be saved, that Ivan had won by default.

His palm stopped its arousing circling and rested over her heart. "It's beating like a frightened bird," he murmured. "Are you afraid of me, Alyson?"

Unable to speak, she shook her head slowly. "Good," he whispered, his breath fanning her cheek. "Because I want you to enjoy this as much as I shall. I would never do anything to hurt you."

His head was lowering far too slowly for her. With a moan that spoke of her intense frustration, she cupped his face and pulled it down for the kiss her mouth was crying for. He resisted for a second. Then, with smile telling of his triumph, he accepted her gift. He clasped her shoulders, holding her body inches from his while he plundered for the sweet treasure that she offered him.

Alyson reveled in the soft agressiveness of his tongue as it searched each tender crevice. When satisfied with that, he urged her tongue into an erotic foreplay, circling, thrusting, rubbing, until she pressed against him.

Seeking his support, her body arched to his, quivering with the need to meld against him, to draw sustenance from his strength to prevent her collapse. Perversely he held her away, their only contact the searing binding of their mouths.

Moans swelled in her throat as her body arched and twisted, seeking its nesting place, knowing there would be no peace for her until his sinewy body extinguished the growing fire. It was as if he knew that by denying her aching need, her body was increasing its demand until she was driven to a feverish pitch.

Slowly he released her mouth. "Your bedroom?"

he questioned, nodding to the door she had closed with provocative glee minutes before.

"Yes," she whispered, not caring that her aroused passion was exposed to his quick scrutiny or that his expression showed his supreme satisfaction that she was accepting his domination at last.

Monsieur X, may I introduce you to Ivan Kyriokos. The thought caused a giggle to waver in her throat when he opened the door and they entered her bedroom. How many fantasies did one have that came to life in such red-blooded, living color?

Then she was pulled into his arms and her frivolous thoughts were lost as moist kisses moved heatedly over her face and down her neck before finding their home on her waiting mouth. Her hunger to curve into his body was finally assuaged, only to be replaced with a new fire as his masculine arousal was manifested to her.

His hands caressed the clinging silk covering her back as he pressed her close. They moved over every curve of her body as if checking how they fit in the spread of his hands. His mouth, too, resumed its search, tasting, licking, nibbling her cheeks, her ears, her neck.

Her head found the delight of his shoulder, and she pushed his open shirt away impatiently so she could perform her own investigation. The slightly salty taste of his skin was an aphrodisiac, and she nuzzled into and licked the warm curve before traveling over his bared shoulder. She tugged impatiently at his confining shirt until he shrugged it off.

The zipper whispered on her jump suit. It was kicked off when it slid to her ankles. "My God, you're beautiful!" he murmured in awe as he held her at arm's length by her shoulders.

She stood unabashed as his heated gaze swept over her hard-tipped, pointed breasts, her nipped-in waist and the long sweep of her slender legs. She was swept into his arms and led to the bed. Then he bent to remove the cover, pausing to run his fingers lingeringly over the spread.

"Velvet!" he chuckled with delight. "You sensuous witch! How perfect for our love!" He pressed her backward, their naked bodies tingling in voluptuous anticipation upon making contact with the lush softness of the material.

The mattress sagged slightly as he settled next to her, and Alyson wondered if there could be a more erotically stimulating sensation than knowing a man was causing that shifting of one's bed.

Her arms opened to him and he moved to her, caressing her tenderly. His mouth continued its foray. Now that there were no obstructions, her body arched and twisted under his kisses. She thrilled at his trembling when her mouth discovered his erogenous areas. She found he was right about the velvet bedspread. With every movement the silky texture stimulated her sensitized flesh further. It was as if she were being stroked by mink-gloved hands.

Thrilling to the way he responded to her first timid caresses, she soon became bolder, sensing his delight in her exploration. Never had she touched a man's body like this before, nor had she had the desire. But the more he gave her pleasure, the more she wanted to return the gift.

She didn't know a man's body could be so seductive. The combination of the muskiness he exuded and the expensive toilet water he used was heady. She loved the roughness of his chest hair and the way it stimulated her newly sensitized fingers. A moan of pure pleasure erupted when it brushed her hardened nipples. She discovered that his body was as strong as she'd envisioned, that the sinewy muscles that tensed in response to her manipulation were firm and hard.

Even as she marveled over her delight at each new discovery of his body, her own was being inflamed by his equally searching mouth. His wonderfully gentle yet probing fingers prepared the way for the moist invasion of his tongue. Lower and lower he went until his hands trailed the outer curve of her thighs and made the slow return along the ultra-soft flesh lining the inner curve.

"Ivan . . . please!" His name rose in an anguished plea, rising from deep within the tormenting ache engulfing her. With a groan he surged over her, taking her mouth again in a long kiss. His hair-roughened thigh parted hers and she slid under him for the final act that would make her his.

The unbidden thought startled her, but it was swept away as his hand cupped her buttocks to position her, and she accepted him into the warm moist inner core of her womanhood. She was complete at last.

She matched his slow rhythm until unable to wait any longer. Her fingernails dug into his shoulders in protest over his teasing. It was the response that he'd been waiting for. She rode the wild thrusting, opening and giving of herself until they exploded in a glory of starbursts, and she clung gasping to him while he carried her safely back from newly explored outer space.

He covered her face with a layer of light kisses, murmuring Greek words of love that seemed more beguiling to her for not knowing their exact meaning. When their bodies cooled, he pulled the two sides of the bedspread over them, encasing them in the velvet covering. She marveled over his sensuality.

"Are you all right, *agape mou?*" he questioned, pulling her into the circle of his arm.

"Mmm," she confessed sleepily, loving the sound of Greek endearment. She turned slightly to place a kiss over his heart.

"Then rest, because I'm warning you that after that sampling I'll be wanting more," he murmured in teasing warning.

"Sampling!" she cried in indignation, half rising.

Laughing, he pulled her back against his body. "Hush, sweet one," he whispered. "You're like a very delicious treat, the kind that brings a man back to want another taste."

His hands moved soothingly over her back, pressing her close. The long fingers slid over her rib cage and breasts, lingering as if to reassure him of their perfection before moving on. They traveled in slow circles over her taut abdomen before finding the soft juncture of her thighs.

Dual quivers ran through them and he shifted to move over her and take her mouth. "The time for tasting seems to have arrived sooner than expected," he whispered with a rising urgency.

Their lovemaking took a new dimension as they retraced each other's pleasure points with leisurely delight. Again they climbed, then raced, to the pinnacle, only to cling together as they tumbled down in cloud-soft repletion after reaching their goal. Their kiss was a paean in homage to what they had just shared, and the melody stayed with her as she floated into a deep sleep.

* * *

The sky was pearl gray with the beginning of dawn when Alyson drifted into wakefulness. She stretched with feline grace, and the unaccustomed ache to her limbs brought a smile to her lips when memory flooded her.

"Such satisfaction! May I be presumptuous and assume that I'm the cause?"

Alyson's eyes flew open to find Ivan standing by the bed. The sound of the shower must have awakened her, for he was rubbing his wet hair with a towel. He stood unabashed in his nakedness while smiling down at her, and her insides quivered in response. That same body had transported her to unsuspected heights of ecstasy throughout the night, and she stared at him frankly, marveling at his beauty.

He bent over the bed to kiss her lids closed. "If you keep looking at me like that I'll never get to my nine-o'clock appointment," he warned.

Her hands slid down his side and over his hips, tugging him down beside her. "Is it that important?" she murmured seductively.

"Insatiable hussy," he returned. His smile showed his pleasure at her act, but he placed a firm kiss on her lips before rising with evident reluctance. "Do you think I'd be leaving if it weren't so?" He stroked her naked breasts with arousing fingertips. The velvet in his eyes receded to show the barely banked fires while he watched with fascination as the rosy tips peaked in anticipation.

"I'm experiencing something new," he admitted in husky wonder. "I find that my hunger hasn't been satisfied, and I'm wondering if even a month in your arms would be enough."

He bent once more to nip at the inviting buds before

soothing them with a moist kiss. "Lovely," he said under his breath, then moved to her lips. He captured her hands before she could lure him with her touch and held them firmly until he was finished with the kiss.

He nuzzled his face in her hair and surprised her with his question. "Tell me, what perfume are you using? It's been haunting me."

Alyson chuckled throatily, amusement lighting her eyes. "It's something new—based on a pheromone that's supposed to be irresistible to the opposite sex."

"I'll have to send them an affidavit attesting to their success!" he growled while nipping her earlobe.

Their laughter blended and his mouth took hers in a final kiss. "I'd better leave now before I forget all else and decide to start that month right now," he said, tousling her hair before retreating to the safe distance where his clothes were draped on a chair.

Alyson offered to make Ivan breakfast, but he declined with a smile and a shake of his head. "I find you far too tempting right now. Go back to sleep, sweet one. I'll be in touch."

He shrugged into his handsome gray silk jacket and gave her a final farewell kiss before striding from the room. Alyson curled into the velvet spread, the smile on her lips telling of her satiated happiness. Obeying his dictate, she fell asleep immediately, purposely refusing to contemplate the vagueness of his promise about a future meeting.

7

~~~~~~~~~~~~~~~

Alyson made a face at the silent phone. What did she expect? she berated herself. All her fine intentions about not falling into Ivan's arms, of refusing to become another casualty of his Greek charm, had gone down the drain. All he'd had to do was lift his imperious finger and she'd forgotten about her resolve not to become another name on his list of pillow friends. She had succumbed, and as she'd suspected and now knew, he couldn't care less after such a swift conquest.

"I'll be in touch," he'd said, and as a result she had been afraid for the past three days to leave the house in case the call came while she was out. She had no one to blame but herself. He hadn't coerced her. But damn it, it hurt to discover she'd given so completely of herself and all that she'd received in return was the practiced expertise of an accomplished womanizer.

How could she have deceived herself into thinking

that something special had happened between them? What made her think she had anything more to offer than what he got from his other affairs?

Thoroughly exasperated with herself, Alyson pushed her hand through her already tousled hair. Thank goodness she had only one night to get over and forget. But what a night! the aching part of her that remembered cried in protest.

Fortunately she'd soon be in Ecuador, hundreds of miles from any further devastating encounters. His lovemaking was much too potent for her. Another dose might well create a craving that could be difficult to get over.

She moved restlessly through the living room, forcing herself to consider how strange it was that there'd been no contact made about the flight south. She'd received the promised postcard from Bob when he'd passed through the Panama Canal, so she knew at least that the *Semele* was proceeding on schedule. Except by contacting Ivan, which she refused to do, she had no way of ascertaining the date of her own departure.

The past three days had been spent cleaning the condo and packing the rest of her clothes. She kept minimal food in the house and found day-to-day living, not knowing when she would be expected to leave, very frustrating. It didn't help nerves already frayed by Ivan's neglect.

Her restlessness drove her to slip into a two-year-old bikini and, scrub pail in hand, march out to wash the car. It was there, wet with the spray from the hose, that a neighbor approached her and invited her to the barbecue that the condo complex was having that night. She didn't care for the way his eyes were lapping over her, but she decided there'd be safety in numbers, and anything was better than the TV dinner that was all that her freezer had to offer.

She finally convinced her neighbor that the party was not going to begin at once in either his place or hers, and he left with a little-boy pout that almost made her decide not to go. What a child he seemed after the heady meeting of mind and body she'd been fortunate to have experienced with Ivan.

The operative word was *fortunate*, she admitted while winding the hose in place. There should be no regrets after the mind-expanding pleasure that had been discovered in Ivan's arms. She suspected that in the future there'd be few men who could equal his expertise, but that would be her problem for expecting too much.

Alyson found herself enjoying the party once her neighbor was convinced that she didn't consider him as her date. He soon found a more amenable divorcée who was willing to smooth his ruffled feathers. Alyson was left to circulate through the group and talk to neighbors her frequent absences had made difficult to meet.

When returning home, she heard her phone ringing and dashed the remaining yards. Muttering frustrated imprecations while fumbling for her key, the door was finally opened as the instrument gave its last ring.

Her knuckles were white around the receiver. Why was she so certain that it had been the awaited call from Ivan? It was after nine. He certainly wouldn't call so late, especially after letting three days go by without any communication.

She shook her head at her persistent and foolish hope. Ivan had greener pastures to investigate, other conquests to make. It was time to accept that hard fact.

She was managing to control her daydreams. The next project was to banish those that were invading her nights.

Precisely one half hour later the phone rang again. Alyson flew to it and, pausing only to take a controlling breath, plucked it from its cradle.

"Miss O'Hare?" She swayed upon hearing the accented voice. Dear Lord, was she that far gone that he could affect her at this distance? she thought in alarm, even as disappointment flooded her. The voice was not Ivan's.

She cleared her voice with an effort when she recognized his servant. "Yes, Giorgio. Is there something I can do for you?"

"I received instructions from Mr. Kyriokos this evening to contact you every half hour until you answered. He tried getting to you earlier but you were out."

Double damn! She knew she shouldn't have gone to that stupid party! "Oh?" she said with studied indifference. "He couldn't try again?"

"He's been very busy in New York for the past three days," Giorgio replied patiently. "I'm to tell you that a limousine will come for you tomorrow at noon to take you and your luggage to the airport. Will you be able to be ready?"

Just like that! she stormed. No warning—just jump! But her relief that she was finally getting on her way quickly modified her initial resentment. She'd been concerned about leaving her car at the airport, and had even checked into a taxi service to pick her up, but this was the ideal solution.

Having seen indications of Ivan's efficiency, she shouldn't be surprised that he'd given thought to her transportation. He'd always insist on complete control of whatever project he was involved in and see to the slightest detail.

"I'll be ready," she promised. Giorgio hung up before she could ask how many others would make up the party. She gave a faint shrug. Tomorrow would bring her answers.

When preparing for bed, Alyson used the knowledge that Ivan had been in New York as a plausable excuse for not hearing from him. She tried to quell the lingering hope that she might still see him once more with the fact that by the next evening she'd be several hundred more miles out of his orbit.

Alyson had closed the house innumerable times, so it took little effort to be ready the next day. By the time the black limousine stopped in front of her door at precisely noon, she had made her last inspection and was ready with her bulky camera case, a suitcase and carry-on at her feet.

The chauffeur was young and, after casting an appreciative glance over her, hurried to deposit her cases in the trunk. For the long trip Alyson chose to wear a navy pantsuit, its somber color relieved by a striped scarlet blouse. The outfit had proven its value before. It was remarkably wrinkle-resistant under trying conditions. This would be her first contact with the rest of the crew, and she knew first impressions were the ones that lingered.

She leaned back, enjoying the lush interior as the car sped to the airport in Miami. Her mind was captivated with thoughts of the country she would soon be visiting, and she barely noticed the passing scenery.

Ecuador. A scant month before she hadn't even been quite certain about its location in South America. Now she'd be spending a whole summer there, helping with the photography and numbering the artifacts they hoped to bring up from a centuries-old grave on the Chanduy Reefs off its coast.

Bob had shown her the report of the previous year's testing. One of the chief problems was the cold current that swept off its shores. It was rich in nutrients, which was the reason for the thriving fishing industry. But the prolific fish also brought sharks, the report read, and sea snakes. Sharks she had learned to live with, but sea snakes she could do without.

Other problems would be the limited vision in the silted water and the abundance of long strands of seaweed, which could wrap the unwary diver into a bondage that was always difficult to cut out of.

In spite of those difficulties, they had managed to locate the wreck that gave every indication of being the long-sought-after *Santa Teresa*. Alyson was impressed by the obvious expense of the operation, and was thankful that Ivan seemed able to keep the project going until he was satisfied they'd hauled up all the treasure . . . or that once again the sea had the last laugh by refusing to give up what she had claimed.

Alyson had been so certain that the Miami International was their destination that she gave a start of surprise when the car turned into the nearby Opa-Locka Airport. She knew it was a base for private planes, and therefore managed to camouflage her further surprise when a man, his uniform showing the double stripes of a co-pilot, came from the glass-fronted building to open the door.

"Miss O'Hare?" he asked pleasantly. "I'm Joe Crampton. I'm glad you arrived on time. We'll be taking off in half an hour. Will you follow me and come on board?" He offered his hand to help her out of the car and angled his head to the chauffeur, indicating the Lear jet sitting in front of the building, where he was to take her luggage.

The wind whipped at her as she went up the short flight of steps and moved into the sleek jet. Lears, she knew, were to the smaller noncommercial planes what Roll-Royces were to other cars. Ivan's financial resources were boundless if he could place this type of accommodation at the disposal of the rest of the search team. She had expected a tourist-class ticket on an intercontinental run.

She was introduced to the pilot, Jim Douglas, his broad smile welcoming her aboard. He held a clipboard while going through the preflight check necessary before the plane was wheeled to the runway.

Joe indicated a seat by the window, and Alyson looked around the body of the plane with interest. It was decorated in the rich royal blue and white that seemed to be Ivan's favorite colors. There were a half-dozen comfortable chairs, and while bolted down, they could be angled and turned into various positions. She was surprised that, with the takeoff time so near, she was the only passenger aboard.

"Would you like something to drink?" Joe asked after showing her the levers controlling the seat. "We have a well-stocked bar and coffee or tea, hot or cold."

"Iced tea would be fine," Alyson said. The larder had been empty at home. She had assumed that lunch would be served on the plane and hadn't eaten, and her stomach was letting her know how empty it was. Breakfast had been the last slice of bread, toasted and spread with the scrapings from the jelly jar, and a cup of black coffee, since the milk had been finished the day before. It had been a decidedly frugal repast, and she now wondered if she'd have to wait until they reached Ecuador before getting her next meal.

Joe placed the iced tea on a side table that he hooked onto the arm of the seat. A small bowl of potato chips followed. When he excused himself to go forward to assist in the preflight check, she quickly ate the snack.

She had just crunched the last salty chip when both the pilot and co-pilot came to attention and hurried to the open hatch. Alyson's seat was on the side of the plane away from the building, so she couldn't see how many were coming on board. Her attention was focused on the opening with an anticipatory smile of welcome.

Her lips parted in a surprised "Oh!" when she saw a tall, sinewy figure fill the doorway, and a thrill of pleasure raced through her. Was Ivan coming to bid them farewell as he had the crew on the *Semele*?

"Welcome aboard, Mr. Kyriokos," Jim said with a smile. "I checked the tower when I saw you arrive. We can take off as soon as you're fastened in."

Ivan shook hands with the men. "Fine. We'll take our seats immediately. You know my aversion to wasting time in an airport." He stepped into the plane and Alyson's surprise was compounded upon seeing Giorgio and Sylvos, his secretary, behind him.

Only then did Ivan turn to look at Alyson, and his smile took a mocking curve. "You look surprised, Miss O'Hare. Who did you think was coming on board?"

Her mouth gaped as she struggled to get over her initial shock. "The rest of the crew, of course! Where are they?"

He gave a dismissive shrug before taking the seat next to her. "They leave in three days. By then I shall be finished with my appointments in Mexico City, and we'll be in Guayaquil to meet them when they arrive."

"I don't understand!" Alyson protested. But she did, and most definitely didn't care for his manipulation. She started to release her seat belt when his hand stayed her action.

"Relax, Alyson," he admonished firmly. "You're not going anywhere."

The fact was driven home when she saw the boarding ladder being retracted and Jim throw the bar to latch the door shut. Giorgio smiled politely as he removed her empty glass and the bowl in preparation for lift-off. The jet engines roared to life and the two men took seats in the back. The plane gave a slight shudder and was maneuvered into position on the runway. Joe called the alert, and the engines revved up into a whine. The takeoff was smooth, and seconds later Alyson saw the varied blues of the Atlantic Ocean beneath them before the plane made a slow arc and headed back overland and toward the Gulf of Mexico.

It was a clear day, and the strand of keys curved off the tip of Florida like the dot-dash of a message in erratic Morse code. When the blue waters of the Gulf were playing hide and seek through the puffy cumulus clouds, Alyson turned accusingly to Ivan.

"You do know that you're leaving yourself open for a kidnapping charge," she threatened. "It would be wisest for you to book me through to Guayaquil as soon as we land in Mexico City." How dare he assume she'd go along with his cheap trick! Did he really imagine that he could ignore her for three days and then think she'd fall willingly into his arms? If he needed a bed companion, he'd have to resort to finding a senorita. His business acquaintances would be all too eager to assist him in the hunt, she concluded waspishly.

"I had Giorgio make certain there was Campari on board for you, since you seem to enjoy it," Ivan said, ignoring her outburst, and flicked his finger to the man standing behind them.

Still tending to details, she groused scathingly, resentful over the way his thoughtfulness was causing her anger to crumble. It was no wonder he was able to amass his wealth if he manipulated his clients with the same practiced ease.

The drink was placed on her small table. A martini was set on another table snapped onto Ivan's armrest. By the time her glass was emptied, humor replaced her initial anger and a smile formed, replacing her scowl. She'd been irked by his lack of communication after saying he'd be in touch with her. He certainly did things with a flair, if getting in touch meant whipping her off to a rendezvous in Mexico City.

"I see by your smile that I'm forgiven," Ivan murmured with satisfaction. "When we first met, I knew you were a woman who could rise to any situation with your humor intact."

"Especially when I have a Lear jet underneath me," she returned dryly.

He threw back his head and gave a full-throated laugh. Her gaze focused on the exposed bronzed column. Memories tingled messages as she recalled how his warm flesh had tasted when she'd nuzzled along its curve.

Appetizing aromas came from the small galley tucked in the rear of the plane. Lunch was finally served, not on plastic dishes, but on fine china bordered in blue to match the decor of the interior.

Traveling with Ivan was to travel in high style. Alyson became somber at the thought.

Everything about this man could become habit-forming, and that was where the danger lay. She liked watching the way he walked, his stride matching his forceful personality. She enjoyed talking with him, his intellect stimulating her to meet him on an equal basis. It gave her great pleasure when she was able to make him laugh or succeeded in teasing him—not to mention the fact that in his arms she'd touched the stars.

The combination enticed her. Would Mexico City prove a disillusionment, or would she be tempted further by his charms? Careful, warned the remnants of her common sense. Ivan leaned over to open her napkin and lay it on her lap, and that sterling little voice had no chance against the sensations rippling through her when the back of his hand brushed the underside of her breasts.

After the delicious meal of cold vichyssoise and trout almondine with a delicate lemon-butter sauce, followed by a selection of cheeses and fresh fruit, Giorgio offered her a choice of magazines. Ivan and Sylvos became immersed in the intricacies of the pending meetings, conversing in Greek over the papers extracted from the secretary's case. She glanced idly through the pages, still bemused by the unexpected turn of events.

Alyson rested her head on the back of her seat and closed her eyes. She sighed when she realized that the silken fibers of the net Ivan was weaving might have already made any rebellion useless. Her eyes drifted open to see him turning after catching the faint sound that she made.

"Tired?" he queried softly. "You must excuse us for

speaking in Greek, but we can cover this preliminary work more swiftly if we use our native tongue."

"I understand," she replied, a mischievous glint in her eyes. "Besides, any technical talk would be all Greek to me anyway!"

"Minx!" he laughed. "I'll give you something you can relate to. We're invited to a formal reception tonight. I doubt that you brought along an evening gown, so that delightful mind of yours can decide what we shall buy later."

Alyson stiffened in her seat and glared at him. "No, thank you. I'd rather not go." Did he really think she'd accept expensive gifts from him?

His gaze iced over. "The outfit you have on, while attractive, will hardly be acceptable at the dinner. Let's hear no more of this nonsense." He closed the subject by turning back to the discussion with his secretary, leaving Alyson steaming in her private rebellion.

The stinker knew that she wouldn't lower herself by arguing before the others, but he'd get her message if he dared press the subject later! She drew the line on his buying her clothes—or anything else for that matter. She was willing—no, needed—to explore further the attraction that flamed between them, but she refused to have it tinged with the specter that he was paying for her services.

That hateful thought burned her, negating whatever anticipation she had harbored. Not until the co-pilot alerted them that they were approaching the airport did she emerge from her bitter introspection and saw that they were over land.

Sylvos gathered the papers under discussion and went to the back with Giorgio to buckle into their seats. She shouldn't have been surprised upon land-ing to find a large limousine waiting for them or, later, at the luxury of the hotel suite. There were two bedrooms. When Ivan signaled the porter to place their bags in the larger one, she knew the answer to the question of his intentions, if there had ever been any doubt.

An exotic flower arrangement on the low coffee table featured waxlike anthuriums. Sitting next to it was a silver bucket containing a chilled bottle of champagne, which drew Ivan's attention. He checked the label before giving a connoisseur's nod of approval.

"A good vintage," he said, arching a glance at Alyson standing irresolutely in the middle of the room. "You look like a bird ready for flight," he chided gently. "Is this too difficult for you to handle?"

Alyson chewed her lip. She was left with the gut feeling that doors were being slammed shut and padlocked behind her. If she wanted to escape back to her safe and sane pre-Ivan life, she had to make the decision in the next few minutes. She raised confused eyes to his, to become bathed in their velvet stroking . . . and she was lost.

Ivan popped the cork expertly and poured the bubbling wine into the hollow-stemmed glasses. "Come, Alyson. Join me in a drink. I've just spent a very frenetic three days in New York and I need to relax before I start all over again tonight."

She took the offered glass and had her first good look at him. Weariness had placed faint shadows around his eyes and deepened the lines by his mouth. It was apparent that amassing a fortune could take its toll. An unnamed sensation rose, urging her to gather him in her arms and comfort him, to press his head to her breast so as to absorb some of the frustration and weariness from him.

Alyson had no idea what her eyes expressed, but a strange look came to Ivan's face as he touched his glass to hers. "To us," he murmured, his accent thickening. "To a very lovely woman who has managed to invade my dreams."

Alyson sipped the champagne. With him concentrating his considerable charm on her, all of the discomfort, the resentment, that had been building up in her during the flight faded. She realized that was one of the dangers of coming under his spell. One touch, one amorous glance from his incredible eyes, and she had no will of her own.

Ivan tossed his jacket on a chair and loosened his tie before taking her hand and pulling her beside him on the sofa. He cradled her head on his shoulder, and they sipped the champagne in companionable silence. When the glasses were empty, she refilled them and nestled back into his warmth.

He placed a light kiss on her temple that she presumed was in gratitude for realizing his need for these moments of restful quiet. His hand moved in light strokes over her arm, but she sensed he was unaware of the movement, that he was taking absent-minded pleasure from the silken texture of her blouse.

It was when they were sipping the last refill that Alyson became aware of the new purpose in his fingers. The stroking was now a caressing. When he shifted and her head nestled in the bend of his arm, so that he could look at her, she was already anticipating his next move.

"Alyson." Her name was a breath against her mouth. He hovered inches from her; she could have counted each disgracefully curling eyelash. "Alyson," he repeated huskily, and her lids fluttered closed as she raised softly parted lips.

They shared the champagne of their mouths in a heady kiss. Three days of abstinence had proved to have been too long. The realization of the intensity of her hunger shook her momentarily before she concentrated on drinking the elixir that he offered and gloried in the fact that his need to assuage his thirst seemed as great as hers. When he finally left her mouth to taste the ambrosia of her skin, the heavy pounding where her hand pressed his chest matched her own throbbing heartbeat.

The fact that she could affect him as he did her added a new dimension to her reaction. She arched her throat for his feasting while her hands busily unbuttoned his shirt. Enchanted by the firmness of his flesh, she explored his chest, running sensitized fingers over the expanse, enjoying the response she got as his muscles tensed when she passed over them.

"Come," he whispered, and then led her to the bedroom where they quickly divested themselves of their clothes. "I should have ordered a velvet cover," he murmured as he pulled back the woven bedspread. His eyes, fluid with memories, flowed over her slender body.

"If you'd told me of your planned abduction, I'd have brought mine along," she teased with a breathless laugh. Her memory flashed on the incredible eroticism of the napped material against their skin and how it had increased their responses.

He gathered her close for a kiss before placing her with infinite tenderness on the cool sheet. Before, the tenderness, the gentleness, that he gave to his lovemaking had come as a surprise. For some unknown reason she'd expected a need to dominate rather than the intimate sharing.

Alyson went eagerly into his arms and gloried in the warmth, the strength, the perfection, of his naked body as he stretched beside her. "You're tired," she said with concern, tracing the deep line bracketing his mouth.

Ivan laughed while rolling onto his back and pulling her across his chest. "Never *that* tired," he teased. He placed an arm under his head to raise it slightly as he gazed with amusement at her flushed face.

"That isn't what I meant," she reprimanded, giving him a light slap on his chest. She leaned over him, her legs curled underneath her. His free hand moved along her curves, testing the silken texture of her skin even as she found pleasure in the slight roughness of the hairs on his chest.

How could she not have liked hirsute men before? she wondered, loving the slight tickling sensation. Her fingers spread so her palm moved fleetingly over his body, touching only the ends of the hairs. She felt his muscles tense. She was unaware of the molten flames building in his dark eyes as she concentrated on the unusual pleasure her performance was giving her.

Her palm continued its whispering touch down the path of hair to his waist and up again. Caught by the heavier tuft under his arm, she circled it with phantom brushes until, with a groan, he grabbed her shoulders and in one swift movement reversed their positions.

"Where did you learn to do that, you vixen?" he cried huskily. "Are you trying to drive me out of my mind?" He took her mouth with a ruthless urgency that told of the extent of his arousal. The invasion lasted short minutes before he regained his control, and his kiss softened into a seduction that had Alyson moaning and digging her fingers into his back.

His hands moved over every inch of her body, molding her flesh, determined to know even her bone structure. His mouth tasted all of her, as if he craved to sip every intoxicating variance. By the time he rose to settle on top of her, she was quivering helplessly from the sensations he had aroused. All mental processes had long ceased to operate as her senses flared into exquisite life. The touch, the taste, the smell, of him—even the guttural sounds that came from deep within him—became the reason for her existence.

With his first thrust she knew the full glory of being a woman. She gave a deep sigh of acceptance, knowing she was his . . . forever.

8

I had fully intended to buy you a dress for tonight," Ivan announced ruefully when he emerged from the shower. He roughed his hair dry with a towel as he strode to the dresser.

Alyson turned from the vanity where she was sitting. Her gaze lingered over him as he stood so wonderfully unembarrassed by his nudity while searching in his leather kit for his comb. She glanced down at the towel draped primly around her under her armpits and tugged at the end to release its tuck, letting it fall to her waist. This was not the time for false modesty. They'd just shared an intimacy that transcended anything she'd ever fantasized about. Her body never felt more beautiful after the adoration he'd paid it.

Her eyes closed, permitting the exquisite memories to flood her. She raised her arms to continue with the brushing of her hair, not seeing how her breasts, still swollen from his lovemaking, pointed in proud display.

His breath escaped in a hiss from behind her. Her eyes fluttered open to see Ivan's image in the mirror. His hands slid over her shoulders to cup her breasts as he pressed himself against her back. "What is it about you, woman, that makes me feel like a sixteen-year-old?" he questioned in a husky groan.

Their eyes clung in the mirror. Alyson quivered to the message his body was giving her. She rose silently to place her arms around his neck. "Ivan—oh, Ivan," she whispered, her kiss giving her response. . . .

"Are you still accusing me of being tired?" Ivan teased her an hour later as he again emerged from the shower.

"No, but if this continues, we'll have to call for more towels," she answered with an audacious leer.

His laugh filled the room and he lifted her chin with a slender finger to place a swift kiss on her lips. "I've never been with a woman who could make me laugh as you do, *agape mou*," he murmured. An odd look came to his eyes when realizing the truth of his statement.

He turned from her abruptly and put on a dressing robe. "By the way, while you were showering I ordered some food to be sent here," he announced over his shoulder. "I know from experience that the contents of the bar hold more interest at these gatherings and we won't be eating until close to eleven tonight. You aren't used to that late hour."

His thoughtfulness touched her, especially since her empty stomach had just given a rumbling signal when she tied the belt of her robe. The trolley was wheeled in shortly and they sat in comfort to enjoy a delicious cheese-and-mushroom quiche and coffee.

They dined on the small balcony of their suite. While his gaze wandered over the panoramic view spread before them, Alyson indulged in the pleasure of examining his profile. After their lovemaking they'd drifted into a deep sleep, and the lines of weariness on his face had faded. She smiled happily at the pleasant thought that in return he might have received from her as much as he'd given.

Ivan arched his eyebrows at her. "You look like a contented cat after licking the cream bowl empty."

"If you stroke me, I'll purr," she agreed in sheer happiness.

Flames glowed in the dark depths of his eyes. "If I stroke you, we'll both start purring," he warned. "I like those little sounds you make when you're in my arms, Alyson O'Hare."

Her breath caught in her throat as she recalled the soft yet explicit sounds that had come from both of them, love talk without words that had been exquisitely expressive of their shared passion.

"When is the rest of the salvage team arriving in Guayaquil?" she asked, needing a change of subject.

Amusement glimmered briefly at her effort, but he followed her lead. "Three days from now, in the afternoon. My meetings should be over early enough so that we can arrive close to when they land.

"But we digress," he said, testing the coffee pot and finding it empty. "My concern is you and whether you have an adequate dress for tonight. I understood your reaction on the plane, but I won't have you feeling embarrassed by not being dressed adequately for the occasion."

Alyson was surprised by the fierceness of his expression and thrilled over his possessive care. "Shall I show you what I have for your approval?" she asked softly.

"You have a selection with you?" he asked in surprise.

He'd seen her one suitcase, so she could understand his reaction. A mischievous quiver tugged at her mouth. Having been intrigued by that expression during her teasing performance at her house, he followed her into the bedroom, lured by anticipation of he knew not what.

This woman had captured his attention from their first meeting and, he was discovering, was proving more alluring with every hour spent with her. It was a novel experience. Since reaching puberty, and with the added attraction of the family wealth behind him, he'd found the female gender a plentiful commodity that he could enjoy and forget. Few had remained to haunt him as she had during the busy days in New York. He admittedly had planned this abduction, as she teasingly called it, with the definite purpose of putting an end to the disruptive effect she was proving to have. He felt compelled to prove that the special passion she'd aroused could only be the result of her enticing performance that one time.

His eyes swept the rumpled bed upon entering the bedroom and he sucked in his breath. How wrong he had been! What he'd experienced this afternoon went beyond whatever he'd known before. Challenged by her complete giving, he found he'd lost all sign of the reserve that had always been an intrinsic part of his nature. If repetition was needed to finally exorcise her, so be it. The thought brought an eager gleam to his ebony eyes.

Originally he'd had no intention of traveling to Ecuador so soon. It made more sense to go later, after they'd brought up something worthwhile to prove their success. When contacting Giorgio from New York, he'd surprised himself when he issued the order to have Alyson accompany him to Mexico. It was proving to be one of his more inspired ideas. His attention was drawn from his introspection by Alyson's graceful movements as she opened the square of material removed from a plastic case.

"May I present my collection of evening gowns for your approval, Monsieur?" Alyson had once attended a couturier's showing in Paris and now imitated the affected stance of the woman who had described the fashions.

She slipped out of her robe and concentrated on her presentation, avoiding Ivan's contemplation of her naked state.

"*Voilà!*" she said, grasping the corner of the material and billowing the shimmering whisper-soft yardage like a conjurer opening his bag of tricks. It was three yards of a crush-proof silken material in a heavenly honey-beige shot through with gold threads.

For a moment Alyson recalled the tiny out-of-the-way shop in Sri Lanka where she had bought it, and the equally tiny French proprietress who had shown her how to drape the yardage in myriads of styles. Because of the limited wardrobe space in much of her travels, it was an ideal answer to the infrequent times a more formal dress was required. The material folded into a compact twelve-inch square and had thereafter traveled with her, to be used whenever needed for an evening affair.

The long edge was wrapped around her breasts, leaving her shoulders bare. "Behold, the tube dress," she announced with an affected French accent, undulated in a model's walk for his approval. The gold threads glittered highlights as she paraded the length of the bedroom. "Simple but effective, *n'est-ce pas?*"

Ivan had plumped the pillows behind him and sat against the headboard, an indulgent smile on his face. "Yes," he agreed. "but I prefer something a little more expressive for the lady I have in mind."

"*Certainement,* Monsieur Kyriokos!" Alyson unraveled half of the material and wrapped the section around her waist in a figure-hugging sarong. "So! A discreet accent to the bustline is more appealing, *oui?*" Her hand fluttered expressively, leading his gaze over the rounded curves of her breasts and narrow waist.

He cocked his head in a lascivious evaluation. "Appealing, yes, but not quite what I'm looking for."

Alyson bit her lip to still the laughter bubbling near the surface. This was fun! He had, surprisingly, joined wholeheartedly in the game she was playing. This was a new Ivan, different from the dedicated businessman or the consummate lover. She found the discovery of this unexpected facet of his personality endearing.

She quickly adjusted the yardage into an Indian sari. At the negative shake of his head she pulled a corner between her legs to fashion ballooning pantaloons, creating a creditable harem outfit. She saved for the last the effective lines of a Roman toga, with an end pulled over one shoulder so a fall cascaded in graceful folds down her back. It was as close as she could get to the classic drape seen on Greek statues.

Ivan's smile of approval ended her show. He rose from the bed and came to her. Placing a hand on her one exposed shoulder, he rotated her for a closer inspection.

"Very ingenious," he murmured huskily. "But will you tell me how I'm to get through the evening, knowing one strategic pull will unravel everything, leaving you undressed and in my arms?"

"Ah, but I'll make certain I have pins at all of the important places," she countered archly, thrilled to catch the fires glowing deep in his eyes. "I won't be able to wear anything underneath but panty-hose. . . ."

"Ehé!" he exclaimed in disgust. "That's one article of clothing that is an invention of the Devil!"

She grinned saucily: (She understood how he felt.)

Ivan's hand crept in tantalizing sweeps to her throat. "You should have a necklace of diamonds there. Perhaps then I could prevent other men's eyes from straying further." His own lingered warmly on the swell of honeyed skin and the shadowed demarcation between them. Her breath caught as she remembered caresses he'd lavished there. "It's late, but I'm certain a phone call will induce the proprietor to open the jewelry shop downstairs. He must have something that will be effective."

"No!" Alyson cried in distress, recalling the expensive shops lining the foyer. She stilled his fingers in their sensual glide over her shoulder. "I can't accept such gifts from you!"

His brows arched in disbelief. Was he assuming he could pay her off as he did other women? she wondered in dismay. Didn't he understand that she gave her love to him freely? To accept anything so valuable would be placing a price tag on herself; the thought was nauseating.

Sensing her reaction, Ivan didn't press the issue. Besides, it was getting late and time to dress. Alyson blessed her easily managed hair. The women tonight would be expertly turned out, and in spite of her protests over Ivan's offers she wanted him to be proud of her and spent careful attention to her makeup.

After trying a gold-tasseled rope around her waist, she searched through her meager supply of jewelry and fastened a round gold pin to the corner of material draped over one breast so that the end fell in soft folds over the shoulder. Her earrings were long circles of solid gold that nearly brushed her shoulders.

Not bad, Alyson decided after a final check in the mirror. She accepted that she'd be unable to compete with the couturier designs, but the effect produced by the shimmering material could not be defaulted. Anyway, she planned to blend into the background, freeing Ivan for the important business discussions that were his reason for being there.

Adjusting a last fold, she turned for Ivan's approval and caught her breath. He'd been attractive in his hand-tailored business suits, but in evening clothes he was impossibly handsome. The white tuxedo top fitted his sinewy body to perfection and gave added attraction to his swarthy skin. The shirt was pale blue with narrow ruffles down the front. The navy bow tie matched the formal pants, which had a satin stripe down the outside of either leg. God, she thought, once the women saw him he'd never get to those preliminary talks he was hoping to have.

"Ready?" he asked as he fastened a thin gold watch to his wrist.

"In a minute," she said, reaching for the perfume bottle with a trembling hand, only to start when Ivan removed it from her fingers.

"I'm just checking the label," he explained, the corners of his mouth pulling down in a teasing smile. "I don't want to have to fend off the hordes if you add modern chemistry to your visual charms."

Emotion rocked her as she recalled the first time they'd made love and his reaction over the perfume she'd worn with its alluring claim of scientifically unlocked sensuality. Her sea-green eyes darkened as his wonderfully sensuous fingers slid over the smooth texture of her cheek. "We'd better go before you'll have to redo your makeup," he said huskily.

Forget the makeup, she wanted to cry, but she reached dutifully for her small purse. "Yes, we'd better," she agreed in a creditably even voice.

"Only because I have to," he admitted. "I have only tonight and tomorrow to finalize several large orders; otherwise I'd forget about them and unwrap that delightful bit of tantalizing drapery."

A limousine was waiting outside and took them swiftly to the hotel where the party was being held. They were whisked to the top floor in an elevator that was kept free for the invited guests. The first things Alyson noticed were the huge crystal chandeliers, truly works of art, their pendants a myriad of prisms reflected endlessly in the mirrors lining the walls. The ballroom was already filled with people, and she was awed by the splendor of the gathering. Ivan waited patiently as she took in the sparkling assembly.

"Ready to face them?" he asked in a low amused voice. "Or are you having second thoughts about the efficiency of those pins?"

"I'm depending upon you to keep a check on me," she whispered laughingly. Upon first meeting Ivan, she'd regarded him as aloof and austere until he'd audaciously nipped her finger in response to her flippant remarks about the trace of lipstick on his cheek. Since then she had discovered that his quick humor matched her own. Being with this man was a delight in many ways.

Suddenly, in a lightning flash of awareness, with hundreds of strangers around them, Alyson realized what had happened to her. She had thought of being in love with this incredible man, but only in the context of having an affair. Now she knew that she'd done the irrevocable. She'd fallen head over heels—the full heart, soul and mind way—in love with him.

Ivan's eyes suddenly narrowed searchingly and she averted her head before he read what, for an unguarded moment, must have been plainly expressed on her face. She longed to hide somewhere so that she could dream in private over the wonderful knowledge that was sending thrilling darts of excitement through her. Now she knew the reason behind the impact he'd made on her, why she'd accepted his abduction. If another man had tried it, she'd have torn into him.

Ivan clasped her arm and led her to the reception line, where he introduced her to a government minister, the mayor of the city and the president of the business organization that was sponsoring the party. Their appearance spoke of their affluence, as did their wives, standing next to them. But none outshone the man by her side, and Alyson glowed with the proud knowledge that for now he was hers.

On the way into the ballroom Ivan introduced her to several couples. "I knew this would happen," he growled into her ear after one man released her hand only after an embarrassingly long time. "Will I have to spend the evening warning others to keep their hands off?"

Happiness bubbled in her, and a coy smile told him how his words affected her. His breath hissed and his eyes again held the same searching quality as he examined her face.

"Let's dance," he said brusquely. "You've met enough people for now." He swept her into his arms, and Alyson realized he was consumed with an urgency that matched hers . . . to be held and to hold. Could he be feeling some of the same turbulent emotions that filled her since recognizing her love?

She rested her cheek against his, content to dream on that possibility. Even if he was enamored for only a limited period, she could exist with that bliss. Afterward . . . ? This was not the time to delve into the future. She was Cinderella dancing with her prince at a fairyland ball. For now that would suffice.

Alyson was amused when later he considered who could dance with her. The men were mostly elderly and magnificently self-centered, impressed with their own importance, but all relatively harmless. While dancing, she was conscious of his obsidian eyes keeping track of her whereabouts while he carried on conversations with various men whose names she had already forgotten.

At eleven, the side doors slid open and a splendid buffet was displayed in the adjoining room. By that time she was thankful for Ivan's foresight in supplying the light meal earlier. She'd lost count of the number of glasses of champagne that had been pressed into her hand. She didn't think she'd had a chance to finish one of them, but she admitted to feeling slightly light-headed.

"I'm afraid I'm going to have to stay over for several extra days," Ivan announced after placing their plates, which filled with their selections, on a minute table they discovered tucked in a cove between two windows. Seeing her distress, he covered her hand with his. "Be happy for me. I picked up several large orders I hadn't expected. But it means that I have to meet with them again so that the proper contracts can be signed."

"Of course," Alyson said quickly. "I was thinking that we'd miss connecting with the rest of the crew in Guayaquil. But then, there's no reason why I shouldn't fly down myself; you could meet me there when you're through."

He frowned while playing absently with her fingers. "These contracts frequently take longer to be drawn up than anticipated," he admitted. "Perhaps that would be the best plan, but let me think on it."

He made no effort to halt her when she withdrew her hand from his, and that small act revealed to her the truth. Her silly castles in the sky came tumbling down. How could she have dreamed that this man of the world had anything more than a passing interest in her?

She picked up her fork and stared in dismay at the heaped plate. Short seconds ago she'd been ravenous, but now she wondered if she could swallow any of it.

She moved the food around the plate while she felt Ivan slipping away from her. She'd seen the phenomenon before so she shouldn't be feeling this hurt. His ability to shunt all outside distractions aside made it possible for him to concentrate on business matters. She had no reason to complain, she admitted frankly. As a lover, he had permitted nothing—certainly not business—to interfere.

"I'll have to do the correct thing and dance with some of the wives," he said after a waiter removed the dishes and poured coffee.

"A wise business practice," she agreed in a low voice. He looked sharply at her, but she was in control of her increasing despair and her expression remained bland.

His fingertips performed a staccato drumming on the table, telling of his irritation as he sensed what lay behind her cool facade.

"You've made a charming impression," he said soothingly, changing the subject. "Any man would be proud to be seen with you. But he'd be wise to remain vigilant."

Alyson cast an oblique look at him and met his smile, a seduction in itself. She nibbled at a lobster tidbit while watching him warily, even while conscious of the balm his words were to her hurt. He was calming her with practiced ease, making her powerless to resent his maneuvering, she admitted ruefully. Was that part of what being in love did to a person?

"You sound very . . . proprietary," she murmured while looking doubtfully at a puff shell holding a greenish filling.

"Eat it; it's made with asparagus and is very tasty," he urged before returning to their conversation. "If you mean that I'm acting possessive, doesn't any man when he's found a rare woman like you?"

Ivan concentrated on cutting a bite size from his filet mignon before glancing up at her, and Alyson pulled in a quick breath under the enveloping force of his gaze. "I'm a very possessive man, Alyson O'Hare. Remember that."

The warning hung suspended between them until Alyson found the strength to square her shoulders and pronounce her own ultimatum. "That works two ways, Ivan," she declared defiantly. "It would be wise for you to remember that also."

His surprise was quickly camouflaged by an amused

smile. "You look like a sleek cat whose fur has been brushed the wrong way." And I wish we were somewhere else so I could stroke it back into place, his eyes told her.

Alyson was fascinated by the vein throbbing at his temple. His formidable control was soon replaced by a look of detached evaluation. She had no idea what he was thinking now, and directed her attention to the plate before her. A challenge and a warning had been given and received on both sides. Only time would reveal the outcome.

They were finishing their coffee when they were approached by a young man, evidently a courier. "If it meets with your pleasure, Senor Kyriokos," he stated, "Senor Fernandez requests your attendance in his suite in fifteen minutes. The other gentlemen he spoke to you about have also agreed to be there."

"Tell him that I shall be happy to attend," Ivan returned. He waited until the man disappeared in the crowd before turning to meet Alyson's questioning gaze.

"This is about one of the new contacts I made," he explained, aloof, his mind already shifting to the intricacies of the meeting. "He's leaving in the morning for Peru and asked if it was possible to finalize our agreement tonight. It should take an hour at the most. Will you excuse me?"

"Of course," Alyson agreed. Evidently in the world of big business, in which time was at a premium, one utilized every available minute. Did he ever long to throw off the heavy mantle, she wondered musingly—to escape into a more relaxed life-style?

"I'll be on the balcony when you return," she informed him. "The view of Mexico City from this height must be spectacular." And also more relaxing.

She was an outdoor person, and the room, while large, was too crowded for her liking.

His attention returned to her and he frowned as he lowered his coffee cup. "I'm not going to let you remain here unchaperoned while I dance," he stated flatly.

Before Alyson could register an objection, he left the table, to return short minutes later with a man no older than she was. He was slim and darkly handsome in his evening attire, and his teeth gleamed whitely in a broad smile of appreciation when Ivan introduced them.

"This is Rafael Fernandez," Ivan said quickly. "I informed him that since his father's request is taking me from your side, he's obligated to entertain you until my return."

"Ah, but this is no obligation!" Rafael protested gallantly, his dark Latin eyes beaming his pleasure.

Alyson smiled her greeting while silently amused. What an immature puppy Rafael seemed in comparison to the sleek greyhound standing beside him with every instinct, every fiber, honed to precision.

An imperious finger raised her chin, and her mouth was possessed in a claiming kiss. "Just stay away from the balconies!" he whispered in warning as he nipped her full lower lip, then eased the small pain with a final kiss.

It was masterfully done, Alyson had to admit with wry amusement. Rafael could have no doubt about who held ownership after that performance.

Ivan smiled over her reaction, and their eyes met in a private understanding. "I'll keep this as short as possible," he promised, running the back of a finger along the smooth outline of her cheek.

Alyson nodded and watched his departure, unaware of her fingers tracing sensitively the path he'd traced on her face.

"My father is very impressed with him," Rafael began cautiously after taking Ivan's seat.

Alyson turned her attention to the Mexican, immediately recognizing him for what he was: an indulged son enjoying his playboy existence. She'd met many in her work. They'd arrive at whatever operation she was working on, looking for excitement when they heard about the dive. Ivan had introduced her to Rafael's father; Rafael had a long way to go to develop such forceful character.

Meanwhile he was a pleasant companion with whom to fill in time. When he discovered her occupation, they shared an animated conversation that carried them through the next hour.

They were dancing and laughing. Rafael brought a humorous story to its conclusion when Alyson felt brooding eyes on her. She turned her head to discover Ivan standing by the wide doorway, his displeasure darkening his face. Her obvious joy on seeing him lit her face, and his features relaxed as she urged Rafael to dance toward where he was waiting.

"Come," Ivan said, taking her hand with an impatient arrogance. "It's been a long day."

Alyson followed him without question. They left the hall, both oblivious to the abandoned chaperon, who glowered his chagrin.

9

Alyson examined her reflection in the mirror with a captivated expression. The crimson dress, a diaphanous wisp of floating chiffon, seemed to swirl with its own life. Never in her wildest dreams had she thought she'd ever wear anything so gorgeous. The long ballooning sleeves were gathered at the wrists by tiny velvet-covered buttons, and the plunging neckline in front and back led to another row of the buttons cinching the material at her waist. The upper part of the slip was cut to the bare minimum, so that through the thin material her golden skin looked like it was shimmering with an overlay of filmy flames.

She'd reached the stage where she'd given up any hope of controlling the mad roller-coaster ride she was on. It had started the moment that she'd stepped into Ivan's Lear jet, and each day the ride rushed her along with increasing speed until all she could do was hang on for dear life.

Tomorrow was the third and last day of this wildly exhilarating escape from daily life. She only hoped her return to earth wouldn't be too shattering.

And Ivan was feeling some of the same madness, she knew with an intense satisfaction. After a night spent in shared magic upon returning from the reception, he'd barely made his early-morning appointment. Although he warned her that he had a full schedule each day, he'd surprised her by returning early in the afternoon. The next day he'd canceled all appointments, accomplishing what he could by phone.

They'd prowled the attractions of the city hand in hand, acting like tourists. Alyson floated on her private cloud, kept afloat by the heat that flowed through her every time their eyes met.

Earlier that morning, after breakfast, Ivan announced that he'd invited a dozen couples to a cocktail party in their suite. It was a thank-you that he usually performed, he explained. Quick calls to the hotel kitchen and bar took care of the food and drinks, and a surprise trip to a couturier house ended with the confection she was wearing.

A smile hovered softly on her lips as she recalled how he'd used his potent kiss to still her prim refusal to accept the dress. She'd turned down a similar offer in the plane, but now, she admitted, the situation had altered. She was committed to Ivan for this short period, and if he needed her to act as his hostess, she had to dress the part. She knew that her capitulation was due to her trancelike condition, but admitted candidly that she wanted him to be proud of her.

The door opened from the sitting room, where Ivan was consulting with the bartender, and Alyson turned from her inspection in the mirror. Ivan's soft hiss of approval sent, as always, little pinpricks of excitement across her skin.

"Do I pass?" she asked, tilting her head provocatively in inquiry. Her heart skipped a beat as she feasted on the shadowed planes of his swarthy features. His formal jacket was pale blue this time, which accented his dark coloring.

"You know you do," he replied, the deepening timber of his voice telling her to what extent. "You look like a flaming torch, the way you come alive in my arms."

Memories surged of just how intense the fire was that leaped between them. Desire rose swiftly, to be brought reluctantly under control. Their guests' arrival was imminent. Could he hear the thundering drumbeat of her heart? she wondered in distracted amusement.

His sensitive hands ran seductively over her arms, the filmy fabric quickly transmitting his warmth. "I was a fool to buy you this dress," he murmured, his thickening voice heavy with his accent. "How am I going to keep my hands off you this evening?"

She leaned weakly against him under the cascade of emotions he could generate so quickly. Her lips softened with promises as she raised her face to his. The sharp rap on the door snapped the rising tension into splintering shards of unrequited longing, causing her head to drop heavily to his shoulder under the weight of her disappointment.

Ivan muttered several guttural words in Greek that she was certain described of their mutual feelings. "Later," he promised fiercely, but his hand was gentle as he drew hers under his arm, and they went together to meet the first arrivals.

If the smiles of the guests and their obvious reluctance to leave later were any indication, the evening was a success. Whenever Alyson saw Ivan enter a serious conversation, she happily freed him from his duty as host by seeing that the drinks were kept filled and the excellent selection of canapés were sampled. She'd always enjoyed hostessing and instinctively knew when to insert a pertinent question to regenerate lagging conversations.

She was warmly conscious of how, no matter how involved Ivan became, his dark eyes searched restlessly until they found her as she circulated from group to group, and a small, secret smile was exchanged before his attention was again claimed.

"You outdid my expectations as a hostess," Ivan complimented her after they closed the door on the last guest.

Something in his voice made her look at him questioningly. He sounded as if she'd been put through a test, and she wondered at the implication. She longed to question him further, but the bartender and Giorgio were there, doing the final cleaning, and she had to wait until they left.

"At last!" Ivan sighed gruffly after the two had finished and left. He clasped his hands behind her waist, his seductive smile warming her. "I thought I'd never have you alone."

Alyson rested her hands on his chest and gazed at him thoughtfully. "Tell me, Ivan, is it true what Senor Remon said when he was leaving?"

The corners of his firm mouth curled down in a slight grimace while he studied her troubled face. "That after meeting you he could understand the reason for all the canceled appointments? You know that's so."

The guest's statement had been couched in flattering words, but Alyson had sensed the underlying irritation over important business being delayed. "Then it's a good thing that I'm leaving tomorrow," she said carefully over the ache building in her chest. "You shouldn't procrastinate any longer or you may lose out on some of your deals."

He stood still for long seconds, his eyes shuttered in thought. "You're right, of course," he said finally. "My wish is to keep you here until I'm finished, but I'm discovering that you're too distracting."

Alyson had to clear her throat before she could continue. "I'll have to check if there's a flight that lands around the time when the others will arrive."

"I'll have Giorgio take care of it in the morning," he said brusquely before tightening the circle made by his arms. Her head tilted back and he took her mouth in a kiss that demolished her with its usual masterful efficiency.

It was time to get off the roller coaster, but for now Alyson hungered for one last ride. Her hands slid over his shoulders to find delight in the tight curls on his head. Her lips moved under his in sweet giving that built with incredible speed into a demanding passion. It became a moot question of who was igniting the fire in whom—they were both consumed by the same blaze. Their clothes became a hindrance that they quickly eliminated.

Their lovemaking held an urgency that was intensified by the knowledge they would soon to be parted. Later, when still drowsy in the pearly predawn hour, they came together again in a languid pleasureful rediscovery of each other's erogenous zones.

How was she going to manage without this magnificent man by her side? Alyson wondered in sudden fright before that moment's painful awareness was submerged in the spiraling delight of their melding bodies.

The thought returned when, hours later, her plane started on its long glide into the Simon Bolivar Airport in Guayaquil. She'd manage somehow, she affirmed stoically. She'd existed before Ivan had exploded on her scene. But that was the qualifying word . . . she had only *existed.*

For three days she'd known pure bliss. Her body had been lavishly adored by a man who knew every form of the art of love; her mind had been stimulated by his equally agile brain. How was she going to manage the intervening days before seeing him again?

Away from Ivan's overpowering charisma, she was beginning to function on a more rational level. Reason told her how impossible it would be to continue where they'd left off when he arrived in Ecuador and they were surrounded by the rest of the crew. Her mind boggled over the thought of the effort it would take to treat him no differently from the way the others did.

Her thoughts drifted back to the last hour they'd spent together. Giorgio's descreet knock had awakened them. Wrapped in sweet exhaustion, the fleeting rebellion was quickly stilled when she remembered Ivan's early appointment and her flight time.

"I'll push my business through as quickly as I can," Ivan had promised as they finished the breakfast that Giorgio had ordered. "Meanwhile, take care on those dives. If we're lucky, you might have something to show me when I arrive."

"We'll keep all the bullion that we bring up under guard," she teased, her restless hands smoothing the lapels of his jacket.

"Do that," Ivan replied with a laugh, and accepted

the attaché case Giorgio handed him. He cupped her chin for a savoring kiss before giving his servant final instructions about seeing her safely to the airport.

By the time Ivan left, Alyson saw with resignation that he had been already receding from her, his concentration shifting to the complex meetings filling the day. She knew better now how he functioned, even while admitting to the sense of rejection it produced.

With his departure the overpowering effect of his dominating personality receded. An odd sensation informed her that a chapter in her life had just been completed. When they met again in Ecuador, as reason had warned her, the close community life that was part of these undertakings would exclude the possibility of resuming their affair.

It would be only proper that he treat her as one of the crew. He need have no concern that she couldn't agree to that. Besides, she had a horror of being labeled a clinging woman who didn't know how to end an affair gracefully. In the past she'd pitied those who tried to breath life into ashes long after the embers had died.

It was this complexity of feelings that made her write the note that she'd placed on Ivan's dresser before leaving. In it she informed him with careful assurance that the time with him had indeed been special, but he was not to worry when he arrived at the site: She'd know her position.

For some unknown reason she ended it with her full name—Alyson B. O'Hare. It was, after all, the official end to their relationship.

Alyson passed through customs a half hour before the plane from Miami was scheduled to land. Neither

Ivan or Bob had given her the names of the rest of the party; while waiting, she wondered if she'd recognize any of them.

She saw her brother just as he spied her. "What are you doing here?" he cried. "I expected you to be flying down with the others."

Alyson bit her lip in consternation. She hadn't anticipated that Bob would be the one picking them up, or that she might have to invent a story to explain why she was already there. "I, er, stopped off at Mexico City," she began, then realized that a slender girl by his side was with him. She paused to look questioningly at her brother.

"This is Lillian," he said by way of introduction. "Lillian Baker. My sister, Alyson."

Something new in her brother's voice made her examine the girl closer as she extended her hand in greeting. She wasn't the usual flamboyant type he was frequently attracted to. Her hair fell softly to her shoulders, the light brown color showing sun-bleached highlights. Her hazel eyes were shyly friendly. She looked like the typical wholesome girl next door, and Alyson liked her immediately.

"Do you live in Guayaquil?" she asked.

"No, my parents live just outside Ancón," Lillian answered, naming a town not far from the villa rented for their use.

"I met Lillian when I had to go into town for some supplies," Bob explained, and the way his eyes moved in fascination over the girl's face told his sister the story. Her twin had been hit as hard as she'd been, and Alyson fervently hoped that he, at least, would experience a happy ending.

"Have you lived here long?" Alyson questioned. Lillian's accent was American, and she appeared only a few years younger than they were. Alyson was hoping to keep the conversation directed to his girl friend so that her brother wouldn't repeat his original question about why she had come on a different flight.

"My father retired three years ago from the Army and, after a visit here, decided that this was where he wanted to live. I came down to help him settle in and somehow never left," she explained. "I found an interesting job and discovered that I liked the easy life-style, especially after the frenetic years spent being an Army brat and never knowing where Dad would be stationed the next year."

Alyson could sympathize with her. She was becoming less enamored with accompanying Bob as he took off on his far-flung jobs. Each time she returned home she found herself wanting to burrow deeper into her nest. One of these days she suspected that she'd be telling Bob that she'd had it. Perhaps, with the arrival of this charming woman, the day was closer than she anticipated.

A surge of new passengers came through customs and they waited expectantly. Her face lit with surprise when she saw a deeply tanned man swing easily into the waiting area. "Do you know who's coming?" she asked her brother. "Dimitri!" she squealed, running to him with hands outstretched.

"Alyson!" he cried, catching her and swinging her exuberantly in a circle before kissing her soundly. "I'll drop everything anytime for a greeting like this." He beamed. "Little did I know when I got that emergency call to fill in that you'd be waiting for me! This is what I call a bonus!"

"You can thank me for that," Bob said, coming up to give him a friendly slap on the back. They'd enjoyed a good rapport when diving in Sicily. "When the boss asked about a suitable replacement when one of his divers got sick, I gave your name but didn't know if you'd be free to come."

Bob introduced Lillian. Dimitri gave her an appreciative glance, but it was clear that his attention was on the tall girl beside him.

The rest of the group assembled with their luggage. Alyson shook hands with the other two divers, Boris Slavanski, a short but powerfully built man, and Lloyd Farington, who walked with a pronounced limp. Alyson suppressed a shudder, recalling reading about Lloyd being caught when the timbers had cracked on an old boat he was examining, partially burying him at twenty fathoms. No matter how careful one was, there was no way to avert some of the accidents inherent in their line of work.

She discovered that the rest of the crew, who would be the backup workers for the divers, had been hired locally. Attempts at relieving the ocean's graveyard of its treasures had been made many times before, and they were lucky to sign on some with experience.

Dimitri made certain that Alyson sat next to him after their luggage was piled in the van. While everyone exchanged viewpoints about the project, she was able to sit back and look at her Greek friend with new eyes.

He was just as handsome as she remembered. His curly hair and black eyes were similar to Ivan's coloring, yet so achingly different. She gazed out of the window with uncomfortably smarting eyes. She'd said good-bye to Ivan only that morning, and she refused to become a basket case from the way she was already missing him.

Once out of the city, the architecture looked remarkably similar to that she'd seen in Spain, with its whitewashed buildings and red-tiled roofs. The younger natives preferred western dress, but the older men in their loose, pajamalike pants and colorful serapes seemed to be posing for *National Geographic*. They were a little over two degrees—about 150 miles— south of the equator, and she noticed that the foliage was similar to Florida's palm trees and blooming bougainvillea and hibiscus.

The road became progressively worse once Bob turned off the main highway connecting Guayaquil to Salinas, the town at the northern tip of the gulf named after the large seaport. By the time he pulled to a stop before the small white building that was to be their home, they were layered in dust.

Elsa met them at the door. Everyone was included in the woman's warm greetings. The delicious aromas that wafted from the kitchen put everyone in a cheerful mood. They were a good lot, Alyson saw with relief. There should be a minimum of friction among them, which was one thing her frayed nerves couldn't handle at the moment.

"The boss just called," Bill said jovially, coming to greet them. "I saw you piling out of the van so that I could report you all arrived safely. He wanted to make certain you made the trip unscathed," he added in an aside to Alyson. "I told him you were smiling, so I guessed you had." His gaze rested on her questioningly, but Alyson carefully kept her smile noncommittal.

"Are you sure you want to sleep out here?" Elsa asked worriedly when taking her later to the shedlike building set about a hundred yards behind the house. It was roughly thirty feet long and no more than ten wide, and looked suspiciously like a refurbished chicken coop. Bob, she saw, was standing by a Fiat and talking earnestly to Lillian, who looked decidedly reluctant to leave.

"The carpenters had just finished their work when we arrived three days ago. I hope everything is set up all right. Mr. Kyriokos asked Bill how it had turned out and he said it looked adequate," she added anxiously while unlocking the door. She found the cord dangling from the naked bulb hanging from the ceiling, and Alyson gazed curiously around at her new home.

To Alyson, coming directly from the luxurious suite she'd shared with Ivan, the contrast in accommodations was a visual shock. Although it looked primitive, the inside was at least clean, she consoled herself. As she had said when Ivan had offered the shed, it was far better than sleeping in a tent.

A low cot was against the far wall, and there was a dresser and curtained corner that evidently served as the closet. A shabby but intact sofa served as a room divider. It, along with an overstuffed chair, constituted the living section. An ancient two-burner stove sat on a cabinet with a small refrigerator next to it. An old-fashioned enamel-topped kitchen table and three wooden chairs marked the eating area.

The last ten feet were walled off, and she was pleasantly surprised to discover that it had been turned into a very serviceable darkroom. That was where the men must have been working.

"They added a bathroom, such as it is," Elsa commented, pointing to a door next to the kitchen section.

Alyson glanced over the minute addition, which had barely enough room for a toilet, a tin shower stall and a tiny sink that she strongly suspected came from a boat, where space was always at a premium.

"You'll be eating with us when I'm on shore," the

woman stated. "But you know how it is—as long as the weather holds, we'll be sleeping on the boat so as not to lose time getting back and forth."

"Where is the *Semele*?" Alyson had been conscious of hearing the waves breaking on the shore only yards from the house. It had been twilight when they arrived, and in the excitement of getting the first greetings over, she hadn't paid much attention to the water.

"She's safely anchored over the wreck," Elsa informed her. "We have a launch to take us to her. That Frank Doran did a remarkable job of shooting the angles and placing her in the right spot."

"Have they gone down yet?" Alyson asked with interest.

"Just to check the set of the anchors and take a quick overall look at things. Your brother got lucky and found two gold doubloons. We're glad to have that Dimitri fellow here. I understand he's the expert on dating those things, though your brother says he's quite sure they predate the *Teresa*'s sinking. Anyway, it was a nice extra to report to Mr. Kyriokos," she added with a beaming smile. "I can only wonder over the amount of money he's invested in this venture, and pray we'll be able to bring him a decent return.

"I'll let you get to that shower." Elsa continued. "Aren't the roads atrocious! Dinner will be ready in about thirty minutes." She left after making certain there was soap in the bathroom, and Alyson hurried to take a quick shower.

The week passed swiftly as they worked hard to finish the groundwork for the excavation. The men laid white plastic pipes in a grid over the sand-covered mound that the electronic readings promised held a wreck. Alyson was unhappy with the limited visibility when she went down to shoot a record of their work, but found that, while the pictures could never be used in a book, they were clear enough for labeling the sections as they were worked.

Her darkroom proved adequate and the small air conditioner was a blessing. Electricity, she discovered, was supplied by a generator that Ivan had shipped.

She heard that Ivan had called once during the week, and she wished longingly that she'd been the one to answer the phone. But she accepted with resignation that he couldn't very well ask for her without raising questions.

Bill made the passing remark that he'd called Ivan to report that they were ready to begin the real work, the laborious sifting, on Monday. The Indian workers, who had quickly learned the intricacies of maintaining the blowers and lines, insisted on having Sunday off to worship and spend time with their wives and children. Bill had to agree that they'd all worked hard and had earned a day of rest.

Bob had promptly commandeered the van and disappeared, and Alyson guessed that Lillian was the reason. They'd been so busy that there'd been little time for private discussion. On her part she was glad, still feeling too sensitive for any probing. Bob, who had treated previous liaisons casually, was surprisingly quiet about his present attachment. It was as if he still had to come to an understanding of the quality of his emotional involvement. Alyson was sympathetic to his preoccupation and wished him luck. She'd liked Lillian from their first meeting and she'd decided that she wouldn't mind having her for a sister-in-law.

Dimitri took the opportunity to whisk her off after

getting Elsa to pack a picnic lunch. "They're a nice bunch of fellows," he stated, "but I'm getting tired of prying you loose from them."

Alyson smiled noncommittally as she climbed over the rocks that he promised led to a secluded beach. It wasn't that the others paid her that much attention, but rather that she had used them as protection. She had responded to his amorous advances when in Sicily, but that was a lifetime ago. She was a different person now.

Since then, she'd met one man who reduced all others to secondary importance. She'd been challenged by the dominating businessman, been charmed by the laughing, teasing companion, been wooed by the tender, passionate lover.

As a result, she was floating in a limbo and felt as if she would be able to function again only when a certain Lear jet arrived. She did her required work, but it was as if she were two Alysons—one who did the daily jobs, and the other who sat to one side watching, waiting, until *the* question was answered. How deeply did Ivan care for her?

The beaches along the Gulf of Guayaquil reminded her of those in Spain. The sand was a light tan and stony for the most part. They walked for a good half hour before they found a small cove where enough sand had accumulated to form an inviting beach. A cluster of palm trees offered welcome shade.

"It seems silly, after spending every day in the water, that I'm taking you to the beach during our first free time," Dimitri apologized as she spread the blanket that had covered the picnic basket as added protection from the heat. "But please notice, I brought no masks or flippers, and certainly no air tanks! This is strictly you and me, a loaf of bread and a jug of wine."

He grinned, pulling off his jeans and T-shirt with a sigh of satisfaction.

"I do hope you've been carrying more than that!" she exclaimed, peering into the basket. It was better than looking at him in his nylon bikini briefs, which left nothing to the imagination. She chastised herself over her unexpected embarrassment. The style was a favorite throughout Europe, and certainly was no more revealing than the bikini that she wore.

They ate slices of melon while they were still chilled. Deciding that the walk had made them hungry, they broke pieces from the crisp loaf of bread and ate them with chunks of a tangy goat cheese. The wine was a native product and a pleasant accompaniment.

Alyson placed a towel against a tree trunk to protect herself from the rough bark. Leaning back, she gave Dimitri a wary glance. She'd agreed to this outing in the hope of resolving the unfinished business that existed between them.

She'd been avoiding him, but that had made his pursuit all the more persistent and obvious. The time had come to rectify the impression she'd left him with in Sicily. It would be difficult explaining that another Greek had supplanted him . . . but what a Greek!

Her expression softened as her mind became flooded with memories of the way her passion had been brought to full bloom under Ivan's artful love-making. While one part of her warned of the pitfalls along the path she was following, another part accepted that she was too deeply in love to heed those warnings.

How could she deny the magic that overtook her when Ivan was near? Admittedly she wanted more than his transient affection—ever so much more! But she was also a realist. While he'd been full of praises for the way she'd hosted his party in Mexico City, he'd have higher demands for the woman who eventually bore his name. Her eyes darkened with longing as she gazed over the wide expanse of the bay. To be his wife—to be the mother of his children . . . !

"Something tells me that I'm not the cause of that sigh."

Alyson crashed from her dreams to the present. Dimitri was looking at her, and the rueful pull to his mouth made her avert her eyes. He was sitting close to her on the blanket, making her shift restlessly.

"I can see that I was away too long," he continued regretfully. "Only a man can bring that look to a woman's face. Is he someone you left behind?"

Alyson nodded, grateful that he was making it so easy for her. "I met him after we returned from Sicily."

"And you love him."

She nodded again. How could she deny it?

"Does he return that love? Is there a wedding soon?"

She was unable to keep herself from wincing. "I don't know. He's attracted, but who can say?"

"I know what you're going through. It's hell," Dimitri commiserated, capturing Alyson's surprised attention. His expression was bleak as he absentmindedly scooped a handful of the sand and watched it filter back into the depression he'd made. "I've been there," he admitted grimly. "All I can offer is that it does get easier with time . . . except every once in a while . . ."

The muscles along his jaw flexed, showing the control he was exerting on his emotions. "Come," he said abruptly. "Let's try the water for a change."

They ran wordlessly into the sea, and when they

started back to the house an hour later, Alyson was aware of a new companionship between them. They were friends, and she breathed a sigh of relief over the easy resolution of what could have been a messy matter.

Dimitri assisted her over a rock outcropping. Their hands remained in a friendly clasp, a sign of the new level of their relationship. As they walked they talked over what they hoped would be dredged up the next day at the wreck site. Alyson was unaware of the dark, brooding eyes watching their approach from behind the villa's thin curtains.

10

━◦◦◦◦◦◦◦◦◦◦◦━

Ah, there you are!" Elsa called from the kitchen entrance. "Come on, both of you. I just put on a fresh pot of coffee." She waited expectantly, holding the door open for them.

Alyson approached reluctantly, smothering her desire to retreat to her room and indulge in her nightly ritual of reliving memories. It was a fruitless and empty exercise in frustration, and she knew that it would be far better to relax in the company of friends.

"Nothing should smell this good!" she exclaimed, inhaling deeply the aromas of chickens roasting and apple pies cooling on the table. Elsa was a dedicated cook, and her meals were wholesome delights. Since Alyson routinely took the launch to shore every afternoon to develop her film, she missed most of Elsa's evening meals on the boat. She wasn't about to lose out on this one.

She offered to help with the tray, but Elsa shooed

her to the living room, where, from the sound of voices, those of the crew who had decided not to visit the small town were congregated. Dimitri deposited the picnic basket in the corner and was one step behind her as she entered the room.

Later Alyson sensed a warning. Her arms tingled as the hairs rose on them. Surprised by the sensation, she rubbed them absently, then felt as if the breath had been driven from her body.

Ivan stood at the far side of the room, talking to Bill. He turned at her entrance and their eyes met across the intervening space. She felt peculiarly light-headed as the room, the people, receded until they were alone—a man and a woman in a private world where no one else existed. Ivan was there! The knowledge became a radiance showering through her.

She had no idea how long they were suspended, staring at each other. It was long enough for Bill to look questioningly at Ivan over the abrupt cessation of their conversation, and then at her.

Bill cleared his throat before speaking. "This is Dimitri, Mr. Kyriokos. I don't believe you have met him yet. Alyson, of course, you know. They made good use of their time off by enjoying a picnic on the beach."

Dimitri stepped forward, eager to meet his wealthy countryman who was financing the venture. Ivan glanced over him appraisingly and then back to Alyson, this time taking in her disheveled appearance.

Alyson's initial joyous response upon seeing him faltered under his probing stare. Her tongue ran nervously over her suddenly dry lips when she saw the icy look in his eyes.

After a small nod in greeting, Ivan ignored her completely and she sank into a chair, too stunned by his unexpected arrival and unexplained rejection to be able to function adequately. She was pathetically grateful when Elsa entered with the tray so that she could help.

Alyson passed a plate of appetizers, but when she came to Ivan he continued his conversation with Bill, ignoring her presence. She felt the temperature of her face rise at his snub. She had expected to be treated as he would the others, but this unexplained attitude had her floundering helplessly.

Bill defused the situation by smiling his thanks as he took another of his wife's hors d'oeuvres and she passed stiffly to the others. What the captain was thinking about that confrontation, she could only guess.

Alyson finished her coffee, not feeling it scalding its way down her throat. The hors d'oeuvres, she knew, were delicious, but it was beyond her ability to eat one now. "I'll leave now so that I can get in a shower before dinner," she said in a low voice to Elsa. Perhaps by then she'd be better able to get a handle on why this meeting, which she'd been looking forward to so longingly, had disintegrated into such a disaster.

She rose, and was appalled to see Ivan doing the same. "Come, Frank," he said to the ship's radioman. "You want that part I brought down for you. I'll have to tell Giorgio not to prepare dinner after Elsa's kind invitation.

"Miss O'Hare!" Alyson was already out the door when the harsh voice commanded her attention.

She stopped in her tracks but didn't turn. She'd tolerated enough of his uncalled-for dismissal. "Yes, Mr. Kyriokos?"

"I haven't seen how they fixed your place. I hope it's satisfactory."

"Very," she replied crisply, and was dismayed to hear his footsteps following hers on the graveled path.

"Have you've seen the inside?" Ivan asked the question of Frank.

"Why, no," he replied after a hesitant pause. "That's Alyson's territory. There's no reason for any of us to go there."

Indignation burned in her. What was Ivan trying to prove with his leading question—that she entertained with private parties? Did he think the others were fools not to notice how he'd pointedly ignored her?

Thank heavens that Bob was so involved with Lillian that he wasn't present to witness this fiasco and that he hadn't probed the reason for her unusually distracted state over the past week. After seeing Ivan's performance, he'd been bound to remember that she'd never answered his question about why she'd been in Mexico City. He'd come up with the correct answer quickly enough.

She pushed open the door and pulled the light cord before standing stiffly by the sofa to let Ivan examine the amenities. Frank leaned against the door, embarrassment shadowing his face. "Cozy place," he murmured, his eyes darting speculatingly between the two.

"It's livable," she admitted between gritted teeth as she watched Ivan prowl the room. He even had the nerve to check the closet area, moving aside the curtain with one disdainful finger.

His nostrils flared when he saw the low cot with its bright Indian throw rug, which Alyson hadn't been able to resist buying. "This is not what I had in mind," Ivan said with a surprising show of anger.

Alyson's resentment increased. What did he expect
—another queen-size bed with a velvet cover? "This
isn't the United States," she reminded him. "I'm
certain that it's the best they could do on short notice.
Elsa offered to have better furniture shipped from
Guayaquil but I declined. Spending the money would
be foolish since we'll be here for such a short time."
Maybe she should have let her do it. Why should she
care what all of this was costing him?

He didn't answer but continued his examination, giving a cursory glance in the tiny bathroom
before stopping by her darkroom. He raised an eyebrow to question if opening the door would harm any
prints.

A short nod gave him permission and he disappeared to give a more thorough evaluation of the
room. "You have everything you need here?" he
asked upon emerging.

"Yes," she answered curtly, then added dutifully:
"Thank you."

His eyes flared a warning that she was too incensed
to heed. On the surface he was acting the concerned
landlord, but she knew him to achingly well not to be
aware of the anger simmering below the surface. After
all, it matched her own.

"You're lucky to get the villa next door," Frank said
hurriedly in an obvious attempt to ease the tense
atmosphere. "It's convenient being close to the operation," he ended lamely when Ivan directed his hardened gaze at him.

Alyson absorbed the information with dismay. Until
now, she hadn't thought about where Ivan was staying, but suddenly she became alarmingly aware of the
house that was only a stone's throw from her place.
She'd seen the roof over the straggling hedge that

separated the two properties, and had assumed that it was another summer house similar to theirs.

Ivan prepared to leave and Alyson followed, anxious to lock him out and thereby obliterate the sight of him. He turned when he reached the door, and before she could step back, her chin was captured in a restraining clasp. She refused to give him the satisfaction of pulling away and met his gaze stormily.

His grasp eased as he ran his thumb over her lips. She despaired over her instant reaction as she felt herself disintegrated under the remembered seduction.

"We have some unfinished business, Alyson B. O'Hare," he warned threateningly, deliberately using the name with which she'd signed her note so that she'd have no doubt about his meaning. "And there'll be no more romping on the beaches with the men. I knew I shouldn't have hired you, that you'd be a disruptive influence."

Anger mixed with her hurt bewilderment as she stared at the door after he'd shut it firmly behind him. What had gone wrong? She had dreaded this first meeting even as she'd dreamed of it. But not in her wildest imagination had she envisioned this unbelievable confrontation.

It had been an emotional day, from her encounter with Dimitri to Ivan's sudden appearance and unsettling rejection. She shook her head against the confusion and decided that the simple routine of taking a shower should remove the salt and sand and, hopefully, some of the turmoil.

Somehow Alyson made it through the meal. There was no doubt who was the dominating personality. In spite of her depression, she could feel the power of the man and the way each member responded more vibrantly under his questioning.

There was no reason for the dull ache that had settled in her chest. She'd thought she'd prepared herself for his impartial attention. After all, wasn't that what she'd written in that unfortunate note?

Ivan left early, stating he'd see them the next day at the site. Alyson followed shortly afterward, feeling indescribably tired and depressed. It was evident that wild roller-coaster rides were a thing of the past. There wasn't even the prospect of a sedate merry-go-round ride, which was a good thing. She might find herself foolish enough to try for the brass ring.

In spite of Ivan's unexplained attitude, she couldn't still the faint hope that he'd pay her a late visit so that the distressful situation could be resolved. In some way she'd displeased him or hurt him. He was a proud man, she warned herself as she wondered sadly if he'd be there long enough for her to find out what had gone wrong.

They might never again be lovers. While she sensed that what they'd shared precluded any hope for them ending as friends, she at least didn't want them to be antagonists.

Only Ivan didn't come, and Alyson had to get up several times to straighten the rumpled sheets under her before she finally fell asleep well into the early hours. The next morning she deliberately caught the last launch trip to the ship, knowing Ivan's keen interest would have him on board early.

This was the first day of the planned systematic search, and she found the men had already wrestled the long vacuum hose into position. She'd counted on them being infused with excitement so that no one would notice her drawn face and the shadowed eyes. She was diving also and couldn't resort to makeup to camouflage the trials of the night before.

She kept her head lowered as she checked out her cameras, and only half listened to the horseplay between the men that was a cover-up for the increased tension gripping them. Everyone was aware that the moment of truth was closing in. They hadn't invested any money in the venture, but they all wholeheartedly hoped for success for the backers.

Bob did stop to talk to her, but his mind was obviously on other things. She breathed a thankful sigh of relief that he hadn't been around the previous night to witness the strained atmosphere between Ivan and herself.

"How's Lillian?" she asked. "I'm sorry not to have had a chance to see more of her." With the uncertain hours they'd been working the past week, the woman hadn't been around. Bob, when free, had chosen to visit her.

"I have a feeling you'll be seeing a lot of her," he confessed, his expression guarded as he watched for her reaction.

She placed her hand on his arm and smiled. "I was hoping I would. I figured my twin had the good sense to know when he'd found quality merchandise and that the hunt was over."

Bob grinned at her approval. "I might be a fool at times, but I'm not stupid." His expression became somber as he tested his air valve. "She's special, Alyson, and I'm lucky that she seems to feel the same about me."

Bill called out a question to him and Alyson squeezed his arm before taking her equipment from her locker. She swallowed the lump in her throat. It seemed that the time had come for the special closeness they shared to come to an end. She felt momentarily bereft and achingly alone with the unsettling sensation that she'd never be first to anyone ever again.

Alyson zipped into her wet suit and tested her airway after Amelio, one of the Indian workers, helped strap on her tanks. She climbed down the ladder to the low boarding platform affixed to the side of the ship, slipped on her flippers and adjusted her mask. Clutching her camera, she gave the alert and executed the entrance roll into the sea.

The cold water felt good, stimulating her system, which was still sluggish from too little sleep. She followed the long white nylon line into the greenish depths, aware from the sound of escaping bubbles nearby that she was being accompanied down. She turned to see who her buddy was and clamped down hurriedly on her mouthpiece before it fell from her slackened bite.

What was Ivan doing there? Nothing had been said about his knowing anything about diving, but after having seen his sinewy physique, she shouldn't have been surprised. The white plastic pipes that outlined the grids gradually appeared through the murky water, and she saw Bob braced within one section, making sweeps with the vacuum hose. Layers of sand were sucked away and Boris and Lloyd searched each section as it was exposed.

The first find was a cluster of cannonballs, and Boris placed a selection in the basket waiting to haul them to the surface. He also found a large shard of a blue and white plate with a distinctive Chinese pattern. Dimitri should be able to verify it easily enough; she knew everyone was praying that it was a pattern that dated from before 1634, when the *Santa Teresa* had met its fate. If it was one that was produced later, they would know that this was not the hoped-for galleon with its fabulous treasure.

She snapped pictures to record the event, then assisted in the search. It was destined that Ivan find the silver bar, and all grinned happily over the first find of any value. The minter's die cast on the ingot could give the necessary proof of the ship's identity.

Unfortunately it was the only bar found, but they contained their disappointment. They were professionals, and they knew how the currents played a large part in the way a ship's contents were strewn over the ocean bottom. The only course was to proceed in a careful, systematic search so as not to skip or repeat an area, which was the main reason for the gridwork.

By the time Alyson used all of her film, they had added to the basket a small glass flagon and several encrusted objects that to their trained eyes looked suspiciously like they might hide sword hilts or gun breeches.

When the cold temperature made her shiver, Alyson checked her watch and decided it would be wise to surface. She signaled her intention to the others and, jerking the rope attached to the basket, rose slowly with it as it was hauled up, keeping careful watch so that nothing spilled.

They were waiting topside for her when she bobbed to the surface, and pored eagerly over the contents of the basket with satisfaction. The artifacts, at least, seemed to indicate that they were over a Spanish ship that had plied its way from Peru. Doubtless its cargo was to have been transported overland across Panama and then to the homeland.

Alyson took the first haul with her on the launch back to the house. Dimitri had commandeered the cool basement for his use and had built a large table down its center. He'd then partitioned it off in imitation of the gridwork they'd erected on the ocean floor. Each salvaged load was to be placed in the corresponding lettered section from which it had come until cleaned and labeled.

"Our first offering is for box A-5," Alyson announced as she lead the Indian who had piloted the launch and was now carrying the heavy basket into the basement.

Dimitri happily examined the find as he placed the artifacts in the appropriate box in the grid. When finished, Alyson assisted him in setting up the electrolysis tanks. After removing the heavy encrustations, metal articles would be suspended in the saline solution in the tank so that the low current could further denude them of their covering of rust. It would finally fall away to expose what had been hidden from view for three and a half centuries.

Feet scraped on the rough steps leading to the basement and they turned to see who the visitor was. Ivan ducked his head under the low lintel and brought in a basket holding more artifacts.

Alyson was immobilized under Ivan's enveloping gaze, and for a moment all was forgotten but the surging voltage that unfailingly generated between them whenever they met. It lasted but a second before the cool reserve returned to his eyes. Alyson returned to her work, fighting the fine tremors attacking her hands.

Dimitri stood next to her and immediately picked up

on the tension between them. He was no fool. He'd been vaguely aware of the strained exchange when they first met their boss the day before. But now, after sensing the electrical charge the two generated, Dimitri pursed his lips. Poor Alyson, if this formidable man was the one she'd given her heart to!

"Are these from the same grid?" he asked Ivan, directing his attention to a porcelain shard that matched the plate from the batch that Alyson had brought. He'd hoped to get some diving in, but they were already bringing articles for him to work on.

After scrubbing the pieces, he held them up to the light. "These are definitely patterns made in China from the late sixteenth to the middle seventeenth century," he announced. "If we're lucky, the imprint on the silver bar you found will help narrow the time slot to before the date when the *Teresa* sank. I'll have to check on that in my reference books. I know it's early yet, but until something is found to indicate otherwise, I'm willing to bet that you hit the jackpot and are over the right ship. But first let's get a radiocarbon dating done as soon as a piece of the hull is brought up."

Dimitri paused, his enthusiasm waning when he realized that Ivan was only half listening to him. His attention was focused on the auburn head bent over the tank as Alyson made minute adjustments. He was confounded when Ivan shot several pertinent questions at him in their native Greek, showing that he could operate on several levels at the same time even though, from his continued examination, the slender woman appeared to hold his attention.

"Are you planning to return to the ship?" Ivan asked when Alyson began on the next tank.

She gave a nervous start at his unexpectedly direct

question. "No. I'll finish this first, then I intend to develop the film that I shot today."

He gave a short nod and turned his attention to Dimitri, who was still sorting through what they had brought. The two men discussed a small bottle with a glass stopper that was fused at the neck. It was typical of the perfume flacons carried to scent the handkerchiefs that people of the sixteenth century used to waft under their noses against the strong odors resulting from poor sanitary conditions.

Alyson left a half hour later. Minutes later she saw Ivan's tall figure taking the newly cut path that led to his house. The thought rose that he'd lingered in the basement deliberately so that she and Dimitri weren't alone together, but she dismissed the idea as foolish.

His apparent lack of interest told her where she now stood with him. For one searing moment, when their eyes had met across the long table, she'd thought herself back in Mexico City, where their glances had met with the same explosive excitement. She drew in a long, shuddering breath. Somehow she'd have to learn how to banish the bittersweet memories. They caused too much pain.

The sun had set by the time Alyson pinned the last of the newly developed pictures on the line that she'd strung across the living room. Only then, while reviewing them, did she realize with a start of guilt how many of the shots featured Ivan. Her eyes were troubled as she went to the refrigerator to pour a glass of wine. Subconsciously he even figured prominently in her work. Banning the Greek was going to be more difficult than she expected.

Alyson moved restlessly around the crowded room. Immersing herself in her work wasn't proving enough protection against the crushing ache that filled her.

She longed for the comfort of her home, where hopefully she could lock the door and prevent any further contact with this disturbing man until she got him out of her system.

If she remembered correctly, Jack, the diver who had crewed down with Bob on the *Semele*, had mentioned something about having done some photography on past jobs. If she left, he could take over. It all depended on how long Ivan remained. If she had to take much more of his cold displeasure, she'd forfeit her contract. From the way he was acting, he'd be happy to see her go.

With the salvage work under way, the men were staying on the boat. Elsa had warned her she'd have to arrange to come on board if she didn't want to make her own meals. Suddenly feeling hungry, she realized she'd forgotten to tell someone to come for her. Too lazy to go down to the dock and light the kerosene lamps in the agreed night signal for the launch, she decided to look through her limited supply of canned food.

Upon hearing a knock on her door, her first thought was that it was Dimitri before remembering that he said he was going to eat on board the ship. Bob, if he was free, would be seeing Lillian. He'd taken a lot of good-natured teasing about how the van already knew the way to her house on its own. Opening the door, her eyes widened in surprise when she saw Sylvos. What was Ivan's secretary doing there?

"Good evening, Miss O'Hare," he greeted her, a smile skirting his lips.

"What a pleasant surprise. Won't you come in?" Alyson asked warily. Was Ivan sending his secretary to do his dirty work and ask her to leave? "You'll have to excuse the mess," she apologized, her hand fluttering to the string of photographs strung across the room. "They're dry, but I can examine them better this way until I decide which ones are worth keeping."

"That's why I'm here," he informed her. "Mr. Kyriokos wishes to see everything you've taken to date."

"Fine. I'll box everything and send them over first thing tomorrow," she agreed. This could be the opportunity to discover the reason for his attitude, but it had been a tension-filled day, and she didn't feel up to coping with his moods at present.

"He said specifically that he wanted them tonight," Sylvos advised her, "and that you were also to come to tell him what angles you took them from."

Alyson looked down at the old clothes she wore while developing the films. They were in deplorable condition, complete with chemical stains. "I'm tired," she protested stubbornly. "I'll have to first shower and change. And I haven't eaten yet. Besides, they'll be easier to examine in the daylight." They used low-wattage bulbs in the lamps to ease the strain on the generator.

"I'm sorry, Miss O'Hare, but his orders were explicit," Sylvos replied patiently. "If you show me how you want it done, I'll pack the photos while you shower."

Alyson bristled over the pressure he was exerting. She *was* tired, and had no desire to spend even a minute under Ivan's scrutiny. After being forced to endure his presence that afternoon, she was in no mood to take any more. Sylvos's glance flickered over her, taking in her incipient rebellion, and he expelled a weary sigh.

"Miss O'Hare, may I say something? I've been in

Mr. Kyriokos's employ for eight years. On the whole it's been a stimulating and rewarding experience. However, since Mexico City, he's been driving himself exceptionally hard, so that he's become almost impossible to work with. Please don't do anything to irritate him at this time. He has been working on, as you American's say, a very short fuse. I'd appreciate it if you'd do as he requests this one time."

His dark eyes held a pleading look, and she became aware of the lines of strain around his mouth. She had no doubt that when in a foul mood, Ivan could be quite difficult to work for. She gave in because her sympathy for the harried secretary.

She found a box in the darkroom that had contained film and piled in the photos taken the week before. Leaving Sylvos to unsnap the day's work from the line, she took a quick shower and struggled into clean clothes within the narrow confines of the tiny bathroom.

She tucked her red plaid shirt into the waistband of her navy skirt and was satisfied that it's tailored cut made her look calm and collected—Which shows how surface appearances can never be relied upon, she grumbled to herself, disgusted over her capitulation. Still, had Ivan's bad mood been because of the short fuse that Sylvos mentioned? Could it be that his business deals in Mexico City had not gone well? Remembering how he'd procrastinated just to be with her, a flush of guilt touched her.

Carrying the box, Sylvos led her along the path. Alyson followed with her pad of notes that she'd made, identifying the date and the position from which each photo had been taken. She planned to get this ordeal over as quickly as possible. With Sylvos there taking notes, it shouldn't take too long. Recalling

Ivan's barely concealed anger, the last thing she wanted was to be alone with him.

Giorgio met her at the door, his olive black eyes showing his pleasure over seeing her again. How nice it was for Ivan be to be able to take his private entourage wherever he went to see to his personal comfort, she thought.

The villa was slightly larger than the one the crew occupied, and the furniture was of better quality. Ivan was sitting in a large easy chair, a martini in his hand. He was wearing white duck slacks and a black knit body shirt, and he appeared so devastatingly handsome that the sight of him momentarily took her breath away.

He looked up when she entered and rose politely to his feet as Sylvos set the box on the low table before him. His gaze was dark, but it was still able to cause a nervous tremor to run through her. Drawing a steadying breath, Alyson quickly controlled her expression. It wasn't fair that just being in his presence could trigger this reaction!

"Thank you for coming on such short notice," Ivan said, his long finger flicking to indicate that she should occupy the chair across from him.

She took the seat and held the pad on her lap to show her desire to get through the business at hand as quickly as possible. Giorgio placed a Campari and soda beside her and left after receiving her nervous smile of thanks. Only then did she notice unhappily that Sylvos had also disappeared. She had an alarming sensation that the stage had been set and the two were the lone actors, only she hadn't been given her lines.

Alyson savored the flavor of her drink and glanced fleetingly at the man across from her. He was leaning back in his chair, his dark eyes evaluating her with a disconcertingly detached look, as if he were wondering what to do about her, if anything.

She cleared her throat nervously. "Shall I start with the first day's shots?" she asked. Darn him, she grumbled, she wasn't about to let him intimidate her! She leaned forward to remove the pictures from the box, but he waved her back.

"When I informed Giorgio that we were coming here, he insisted on bringing along a bottle of Campari for your pleasure," he said dryly. "So, to please the man, relax and finish your drink first."

"I'll have to thank him," Alyson replied guardedly. "I find it refreshing, especially in this warm weather."

He nodded slightly, not answering, and she found herself clearing her throat again. It was impossible to relax under his unwavering gaze, and she started doggedly on the subject that had brought her there.

"Bill warned me about the heavy storms that can blow up suddenly and how vulnerable the Chanduy Reefs are to the resulting shifting sands. As you saw, the water is murky at best, which makes it difficult to get quality prints. However, the main object of these photos was to create a record of the area where they put down the grids. I used whatever formations were in the background as points of reference in case the pipes were torn loose or buried by a sudden fallout of sand. That way they could be rebuilt as closely as possible in their present location."

Ivan didn't stop her when she shuffled the numbered prints into order. A half hour later she discovered that at some point they'd shifted to the sofa so that he could better view the subjects as she spoke about them.

Giorgio announced that dinner was ready as they

finished discussing the last group of films. His timing was so perfect that Alyson wondered if he'd been listening at the door, then chastised herself for being so cynical.

"You'll join me, of course," Ivan invited.

His calm assumption annoyed her until she weighed Giorgio's delicious meals against the less-than-appealing cans of food that would be her lot if she refused. "It would be difficult to say no to one of Giorgio's dinners," she said, and the servant hurried from the room to set another place for her.

Alyson knew she'd made the right decision after sniffing the mouth-watering aromas rising from the serving dishes when the *paella* was placed before them. Succulent shrimp and bite-size pieces of local lobster and fish as well as chicken lay in the rich tomato sauce. She was practically salivating as Ivan spooned the steaming food on the plates, and closed her eyes in pure delight after her first taste.

"Has Giorgio been trained as a gourmet cook?" she asked, unabashedly offering her plate for a second helping of the superbly spiced food.

"No, it's a natural talent that I'm happy to encourage," he confided. "Unfortunately my friends are as enamored of his cooking as you are, and I'm continually grateful to him for remaining faithful and not leaving me. I know they keep trying to lure him away."

"Elsa is also an excellent cook and we're lucky to have her," Alyson said. "But I believe if I were in the class of your friends, I'd do my best to entice Giorgio away too."

"Who said you're not in the same class as my friends?" he asked curiously.

"My bank account does," she answered bluntly.

Their time together in Mexico City had been an eye-opening experience in more ways than one. The life-style he and his friends were accustomed to was way beyond her reach. That had helped her to accept that whatever route their attraction for each other might take, it could never lead to marriage. It was one reason why she was able to resign herself to getting through this withdrawal period. Once through with this job, she could begin the real mending.

"And you think I pick my friends because of their affluence?" he asked frostily. "Just because I've been lucky in building a successful business doesn't give you the right to assume that a person's bank account is important to me!"

She looked at him helplessly. Sylvos was right: He did have a short fuse.

Ivan sipped his wine while the dishes were removed. By the time dessert was brought in, the tension had eased.

"This is *esponjosa*," he explained, seeing Alyson's interest in the attractive dish. A rich, brown carmelized sauce had been drizzled over golden meringue, and when Ivan spooned a wedge on a dish for her, she saw that at the center was a rich custard.

"I'll have to do penance tomorrow," Alyson sighed after tasting the custard's velvet perfection. "I'm certainly thankful that Sylvos practically twisted my arm and insisted that I come." She could have bitten her tongue as she was raked by Ivan's harsh look. Bob always warned that her spontaneous remarks would get her in trouble.

"Sylvos knew better than to return without you," he said coolly, the short fuse again in evidence. "He knows my orders are made to be obeyed."

"And the great Kyriokos, of course, likes to wield that power!" she flared recklessly.

"That's what power is for," he reminded her grimly.

Alyson stared at him mutinously. Her warning system was alerting her that the kid gloves were off. The real reason for demanding her presence was about to be revealed, and she tensed, ready for battle.

11

W e'll have coffee in the living room," Ivan informed Giorgio. Snaring Alyson's arm in a clasp that told her clearer than words that the hour of reckoning had come, he ushered her ahead of him.

She warily observed the stern set of his features over the rim of her cup. Where was the sensuous warmth of the tender lover, the charm of the laughing companion who had wooed her with such single-mindedness in Mexico City? He was again the firm overlord she'd met who ruled with authority from his penthouse in Miami.

He offered to refill her cup. When she refused, he attended to his own. The steaming black coffee filled the room with a rich aroma that brought memories of all those cups they'd shared.

Her fingers tingled with the desire to once again feel the resilient curl of his hair, to rest her head against his chest and be reassured by the steady beat of his heart under her ear. Another look at his implacable expression warned her not to attempt it.

He was not a Dimitri, who could be beguiled, but a man who never doubted his destiny—a god, Dionysus, who was used to living by his own rules. How had she transgressed? she wondered. And more importantly, how could they have been so intimate, and now act as strangers?

A rising resentment flared within her. Whatever his game was, she was having no part of it. The day had been long and tiring and she'd suddenly reached the end of her endurance.

"Thank you for the meal, but I'd better go," she said, placing her cup carefully on the table. "I should check the electrolysis tanks before going to bed."

His eyes narrowed and his expression grew taut. "Is it the tanks you're interested in, or Dimitri? I understand from him that you knew him before coming here."

"He was part of the search team at the dive we worked off Sicily last summer," Alyson admitted, refusing to be intimidated.

"From the way he spoke, he regarded you as a very special part of that team."

Alyson looked at him carefully. If he harbored even a grain of jealousy, she could assume that he still felt something for her and there'd be hope for the relationship.

"And after seeing the two of you yesterday returning from your picnic on the beach," he continued harshly, "I assume he's been successful in renewing that relationship. For your information I intend to terminate his contract."

"Oh, but you can't!" Alyson cried, aghast at the idea. "You have no one else that's qualified in marine archaeology!" Surely the success of the salvage operation was more important than any personal vendetta.

"It's that or *you* go!" he said tersely. "I had originally intended that Michaels handle the photography detail; he can take over."

"That doesn't give me much choice, does it?" she returned bleakly. When she first thought about leaving, she'd soothed her conscience with the knowledge that Jack Michaels could continue with the work, but it hurt that this cold, implacable man could dismiss her so summarily.

He gave an impatient hiss. "Tell me, Alyson, have you slept with him?"

She stared at him with rising anger. "You have a nerve asking that question. Have I asked anything about the women in your past?"

He gave a dismissing shrug. "They were nothing beyond an end to an immediate need. But I know you too well, my Alyson. To go to a man, you'd have to at least feel some affection, which means a personal involvement. I refuse to employ a man who, when he looks at you forces me to wonder what fantasy he's reliving."

His gaze was fierce as his hands tightly clasped her shoulders. "Did you purr in your throat when they kissed you? Were they driven mad when you writhed under them?"

Her cheeks flushed. A new excitement leaped through her as it dawned on her what he was driving at. Was he jealous? She grabbed at that hope with both hands. Something warned her that if ever she was to unravel the mess she'd created, it had to be now.

"I haven't slept with Dimitri," she confessed in an

urgent need to reassure him. "After what we shared in Mexico City, how could you ever think I could?"

She was almost frightened by the intensity of his gaze until tendrils of satisfaction touched the corners of his mouth. "Ah, yes." It was a long, drawn-out hiss of pleasure before the stern lines appeared again. "I hate to seem obtuse, but could you now explain the meaning of that charming little note you left behind?"

Her gaze faltered, dropping to a vague point over his shoulder. Ever since writing it, she'd wondered over her reason herself. At the time it had seemed perfectly logical to try to assure him that she expected nothing more from him, and she stumbled now through her explanation, hoping that she was making sense to him.

"Did you actually think all I wanted was a casual relationship?" he asked in surprise.

"Well, didn't you?" she demanded.

He turned from her to walk to the window and stare out into the night. "I guess I did. At first," he confessed finally. "I was definitely intrigued by you. You were attractive, but there was more than that. You carried an inner happiness that I wanted to get nearer to, to see if some would rub off. And you were independent. I could see you were unimpressed by my wealth."

He turned around and stared at her from across the room, his eyes a deep glowing ebony, igniting the fires that seemed always to lay banked within her, waiting for his torch alone. "And then there we were . . . you and me like it is now. Can you deny the current that runs between us? It reached out to me so strongly in New York, I drove Sylvos out of his mind as I pushed to return."

She was well aware of the power of that current. It

had driven the air from her lungs when she'd seen him coming into his living room that very first day, and its effect had increased with each meeting.

"It had me abducting you to Mexico City. From experience I knew familiarity bred boredom, and I had to get you out of my system."

His long strides brought him before her and his hands clasped tightly over her shoulders. "But it didn't work that way, did it? You bewitched and enchanted me, you made me laugh and act like a schoolboy." His eyes became dark, bottomless pools as his voice deepened huskily. "And we made love."

She glowed as those memories sent tremors running through her in an unending stream. Yes, how they had made love!

"I could see what was happening to me. In a foolish effort I deliberately doubled the number of guests usually invited to one of my parties, just to put you in an unfavorable light. I don't entertain that often, but it is an important part of my business and I was trying desperately to find some way to show you at a disadvantage."

He shook his head at his own folly. "Instead, what happened? All week I've been getting compliments about you. And all week I drove Stylos like a wild man so that I could get here to be with you. And how was I welcomed? I discover that you spent the afternoon on some secluded beach with a man. I watched through the window as you came, holding hands, talking together as if you were lovers!"

He looked suddenly vulnerable and Alyson caught a fleeting glimpse of the anger and pain he must have suffered. Had she inadvertently hurt him that much! How could she ever explain how wrong was his impression!

Her hands crept up his chest and her fingers moved lovingly along the taut cords of his neck, easing them with minute caresses. "Haven't you figured it out yet that I love you, Ivan Dionysus Kyriokos?" she whispered. "Since we met, there has been no one but you."

Their eyes met, and they were consumed in an instant conflagration. Ever since he'd arrived, their minds had been fruitlessly vying for control. But their bodies, their senses, already knew that the exquisite scalding they were now experiencing had become essential to their survival.

His mouth covered hers with a force that bent her head back. Their tongues thrust and danced, two sun worshipers exulting at the altar of the incinerating heat of their kisses.

Lava, hot and enveloping, flowed through their veins. In the fury of their need for each other, they quickly disrobed.

Ivan's hands, hot brands of desire, burned fiery paths over Alyson's body. The couch bent under their weight as he followed her down into the soft cushions. It had been too long . . . far too long. . . .

But just before the thrust that would meld them into one, Ivan paused. With superhuman control that Alyson could only guess at, he took her gently reverently, and their climb up Mount Olympus was a celebration of joy with the gods.

Only after reaching the crest did the flames burst out of control again to erupt into their private volcano, which exploded in a glorious extravaganza of flames. Slowly the molten lava fell back on itself and ran down the mountainside in an ever-cooling stream, and they lay in heated, tangled completion.

They stared at each other in wonder over what

they'd just experienced before Ivan closed her eyes with soft kisses, and they fell asleep from sweet exhaustion.

The cool night air whispered over Alyson, awakening her. The long warm body sprawled partially over her made her senses sing with immediate recall of what they'd been privileged to share.

How she loved this man! The depth of the powerful emotion had her catching her breath. And with a sparkling clarity she was certain, for at least the present, that he felt the same. Marriage had not been mentioned, and she could respect an aversion to that deep a commitment: she could live with what they had for as long as they were together.

Unable to resist the desire, she placed tiny licking kisses along his exposed shoulder, delighting in the smooth texture and the salty flavor. Ivan's muscles rippled in involuntary response, and the long supple hand that lay resting on the swell of her hip tightened, alerting her that he was awake.

"Ivan," she murmured, and his name said everything.

His hand moved upward in eloquent caresses to cup her face. His thumb pressed gently at the corner of her lips, parting them.

"*Agape mou,* my sweet, tantalizing love," he whispered before he took the gift of her mouth in a kiss that made her dissolve into mindless desire.

When he finally released her mouth, he moved over the silken curve of her cheek to her earlobe, the tip of his tongue trailing darting licks as if in need to savor the special flavor of her skin. "I see that I'll have to ask for your resignation after all," he said under his breath while tracing the outline of her ear.

Alyson jerked her head away in shock, but his

fingers twined themselves in her hair and pulled her back so he could further his enjoyment. "I have to leave the day after tomorrow, sweet one. You don't expect me to leave my fiancée behind, do you?"

Her eyes opened wide in disbelief at his words. "Your fiancée?" she finally managed to gasp.

His hands clasped over her hips as he smiled in amusement over her breathless question. "Yes, Alyson B. O'Hare. If I read your responses correctly, you don't find me repulsive. We'll get the necessary papers signed as soon as we get back to the States. I'm not a patient man, you know. By the end of next week I want you to be my wife."

Her mouth parted, showing her surprise. "Just like that!" she snapped perversely. "You've made all the plans without considering there might not be a bride!"

"I'll have your brother flown up for the wedding," he continued, as if she hadn't spoken. Then, noticing the rebellion darkening her sea-green eyes, his expression softened into a gentle tease. "I've come to the realization that a woman who can tear me apart as you've managed to needs to be monitored closely, otherwise I'll never be able to function normally again."

His smile faded, and his dark eyes began their velvet stroking. "Do you know the real reason I wanted you with me in Mexico City?"

Alyson shook her head, unable to speak. Ivan's hands were splayed over her hips, holding her tight in the cradle of his loins, and the sensations running through her rendered her incapable of speech.

"I had made love to this delectable woman on her seductive, velvet-covered bed, and I was left with an indescribable hunger for more. I discovered that I'd done the impossible. I'd fallen in love, and I had a

181

tearing yearning to see what she looked like in the morning across the breakfast table from me. But even more, I wanted to hold her in my arms the whole night through so that I could see what she looked like when the dawn first touched her with her hair all tousled and her face soft from sleep after a night of lovemaking."

Alyson's eyes glowed with her love. She pressed her hands lovingly against his lean cheeks and placed a soft kiss on his lips. "Then I suggest we not waste any more time, don't you think?"

A low laugh rumbled in his throat as he swung from the couch and, taking her hand, led her to his room. "We'll start our life together properly—in my bed," he said with teasing arrogance. "And in the morning, with the sun warming us, I'll kiss you awake. Then, over breakfast, we'll finish our plans."

Alyson looked at him, electrifyingly aware of her body's response. He was the proud god Dionysus, his aristocratic head thrown back in victory. She turned to him when they reached his bed and went eagerly, joyously, into his arms, knowing that soon he would be Ivan, her tender lover, the other half that made her whole.

12

A frown formed between Alyson's brows as she examined the photos spread over the marble dining room table. The ones taken in Ecuador hadn't the clarity she preferred, but she felt that the murkiness lent them a certain mystery. A sigh escaped her as she considered which ones were suitable for her new book.

"Are you all right?" The question held concern as Ivan stepped behind her and wrapped his arms around her.

Alyson's eyes closed in bliss as she leaned back against his strong, supple form. It was sinful still to be so aroused by her husband's touch after six months of married life.

"You shouldn't put that strain on yourself by bending over the table like that!" he scolded solicitiously.

His wonderful hands, which knew every part of her body in intimate detail, cupped her swelling breasts with infinite tenderness before sliding down to circle her abdomen with gentle possessiveness.

"My waist is disappearing. I'll have to buy maternity clothes soon," she murmured with complacent contentment, knowing without looking of the happiness showing on Ivan's face. He was as entranced as she over the gradual changes pregnancy was producing in her body. This growing result of their love held them both in awe.

She twisted her head to place a kiss on his cheek and gaze at him with supreme satisfaction. The arrogant cast to his features would never change. They were inherited. But the contentment, the happiness, she had placed there.

He looked deep into her clear sea-green eyes and gave a small groan as his mouth fastened over hers, and his hands moved with a new urgency. "Sweet siren, you know what you do when you look at me like that!"

She knew. He could still do the same to her even from across a room full of people. "Help me decide, love," she said, reluctantly turning her attention to the prints spread out before her. "I need three or four to illustrate our dive over the *Santa Teresa.*"

"This is a must," he said after a quick review, and Alyson nodded in agreement. Picking up the picture of the engraved rib of the ship, she recalled the excitement that had claimed them all when it was discovered.

The layer of silt that they had at first cursed had proven to be their friend. Over the centuries it had protected the hull and its contents from the disintegrating force of the sea. As the sand and mud was vacuumed away they'd become more excited over the treasures they were unearthing, and when this rib from the ship had been exposed, the telephone call had them immediately jetting down from Miami to join in the jubilation.

After reconstructing the layout, it was evident that the piece of wood had come from the section where the crew had bunked. What long-ago homesick seaman had put that message there? she wondered anew as she read once again the roughly done inscription.

Mother of God have Mercy, it said under an inscribed cross. It was followed for posterity with SANTA TERESA, 1633. The carving had been made the year before the ship sank.

There was now no doubt that they had discovered the correct vessel. Seeing its remarkable state of preservation, Ivan soon had several powerful international organizations interested in raising the galleon, as had been done in other countries. The backers, all having received handsome returns on their investment, also pledged a percentage to its preservation.

"Have you decided where you'll send *Semele* next?" she asked.

"Closer to home, in the Aegean Sea," Ivan murmured while placing small kisses along the curve of her cheek. "I have no desire to fly halfway around the world to check on progress when I have a wife and child claiming my attention."

Alyson turned in the circle of his arms and smiled saucily at him. "Then I'll have to keep our wonderful villa filled with children to make certain I keep you by my side," she teased.

"If that's my fate, I promise to work enthusiastically at the project," he vowed, cupping her hips to pull her tight to the hard lines of his body and alerting her to his desire. "What do you say we get in some practice time?" he purred before claiming her mouth.

It was instant conflagration. Rejoicing over his need, Alyson's hands moved restlessly over the strong muscles banding his shoulders. How she loved every part of this man!

"Come," he ordered, tearing his mouth away to urge her to the bedroom.

"We can't," she reminded him regretfully. "Bob and Lillian are coming."

Ivan scowled while extending his arm to look at his wristwatch. "Plenty of time," he promised. "They're not due for at least an hour. And since they're still on their honeymoon, they could well arrive late."

Alyson's eyes twinkled up at him, remembering their own tardiness and the meals missed. "Did I ever thank you for offering Bob the position of handling your future treasure hunts?"

"There's nothing to thank," he replied firmly. "You know I'm too careful a businessman to do that unless he was qualified."

It was true, Alyson knew. While they were in Ecuador to celebrate the discovery of that carved message, Bob and Lillian had announced their engagement. Later Ivan had offered him the job. Floating in the rosy glow of her own marriage, Alyson had been thrilled for her enthusiastic brother.

When the fall weather brought the dive to an end, they'd flown from Greece to attend Bob and Lillian's wedding. Before that, her time had been spent falling in love with Ivan's island and the impressive whitewashed villa guarded by ancient olive trees; with the large, airy rooms and cool marble floors; with the astonishingly blue Aegean Sea seen from their clifftop, the water vying with the sparkling clear sky. Yes, she decided with deep contentment, she could happily plant her roots there.

They were now back in Miami for several weeks while Ivan concluded various business deals. But now that she was pregnant, she was anxious to return to Greece and start outfitting the nursery.

Alyson snuggled her face into the warmth of Ivan's neck, breathing deeply of the intimate fragrances that were his alone. The wonder of their shared love caused a tremble to run through her. Ivan, ever sensitive to her moods, placed a finger under her chin and raised her face for his inspection.

"What is it, my darling?" he asked tenderly.

Her eyes held a radiant message. "I love you," she whispered. She paused, trying to think how to describe further the sensations he could bring so easily to life within her before deciding helplessly that those three words said it all.

Alyson felt a similar tremor travel through him. Then, with the rumbling laugh of a conqueror, he scooped her in his arms and strode to the bedroom. He was her Dionysus, and her body flamed in anticipation of the rites only he knew how to perform so gloriously.

Practice time, he had teased, and she placed warm, ecstatic kisses along the strong column of his throat. She was so enthralled, envisioning the villa waiting to be filled with children's laughter, that she didn't even hear him kick the door closed behind them.

YOU'LL BE SWEPT AWAY WITH SILHOUETTE DESIRE

$1.75 each

1 ☐ James   5 ☐ Baker   8 ☐ Dee

2 ☐ Monet   6 ☐ Mallory   9 ☐ Simms

3 ☐ Clay   7 ☐ St. Claire   10 ☐ Smith

4 ☐ Carey

$1.95 each

11 ☐ James	30 ☐ Lind	49 ☐ James	68 ☐ Browning
12 ☐ Palmer	31 ☐ James	50 ☐ Palmer	69 ☐ Carey
13 ☐ Wallace	32 ☐ Clay	51 ☐ Lind	70 ☐ Victor
14 ☐ Valley	33 ☐ Powers	52 ☐ Morgan	71 ☐ Joyce
15 ☐ Vernon	34 ☐ Milan	53 ☐ Joyce	72 ☐ Hart
16 ☐ Major	35 ☐ Major	54 ☐ Fulford	73 ☐ St. Clair
17 ☐ Simms	36 ☐ Summers	55 ☐ James	74 ☐ Douglass
18 ☐ Ross	37 ☐ James	56 ☐ Douglass	75 ☐ McKenna
19 ☐ James	38 ☐ Douglass	57 ☐ Michelle	76 ☐ Michelle
20 ☐ Allison	39 ☐ Monet	58 ☐ Mallory	77 ☐ Lowell
21 ☐ Baker	40 ☐ Mallory	59 ☐ Powers	78 ☐ Barber
22 ☐ Durant	41 ☐ St. Claire	60 ☐ Dennis	79 ☐ Simms
23 ☐ Sunshine	42 ☐ Stewart	61 ☐ Simms	80 ☐ Palmer
24 ☐ Baxter	43 ☐ Simms	62 ☐ Monet	81 ☐ Kennedy
25 ☐ James	44 ☐ West	63 ☐ Dee	82 ☐ Clay
26 ☐ Palmer	45 ☐ Clay	64 ☐ Milan	83 ☐ Chance
27 ☐ Conrad	46 ☐ Chance	65 ☐ Allison	84 ☐ Powers
28 ☐ Lovan	47 ☐ Michelle	66 ☐ Langtry	85 ☐ James
29 ☐ Michelle	48 ☐ Powers	67 ☐ James	86 ☐ Malek

Silhouette Desire

$1.95 each

87 ☐ Michelle	106 ☐ Michelle	125 ☐ Caimi	144 ☐ Evans
88 ☐ Trevor	107 ☐ Chance	126 ☐ Carey	145 ☐ James
89 ☐ Ross	108 ☐ Gladstone	127 ☐ James	146 ☐ Knight
90 ☐ Roszel	109 ☐ Simms	128 ☐ Michelle	147 ☐ Scott
91 ☐ Browning	110 ☐ Palmer	129 ☐ Bishop	148 ☐ Powers
92 ☐ Carey	111 ☐ Browning	130 ☐ Blair	149 ☐ Galt
93 ☐ Berk	112 ☐ Nicole	131 ☐ Larson	150 ☐ Simms
94 ☐ Robbins	113 ☐ Cresswell	132 ☐ McCoy	151 ☐ Major
95 ☐ Summers	114 ☐ Ross	133 ☐ Monet	152 ☐ Michelle
96 ☐ Milan	115 ☐ James	134 ☐ McKenna	153 ☐ Milan
97 ☐ James	116 ☐ Joyce	135 ☐ Charlton	154 ☐ Berk
98 ☐ Joyce	117 ☐ Powers	136 ☐ Martel	155 ☐ Ross
99 ☐ Major	118 ☐ Milan	137 ☐ Ross	156 ☐ Corbett
100 ☐ Howard	119 ☐ John	138 ☐ Chase	157 ☐ Palmer
101 ☐ Morgan	120 ☐ Clay	139 ☐ St. Claire	158 ☐ Cameron
102 ☐ Palmer	121 ☐ Browning	140 ☐ Joyce	159 ☐ St. George
103 ☐ James	122 ☐ Trent	141 ☐ Morgan	160 ☐ McIntyre
104 ☐ Chase	123 ☐ Paige	142 ☐ Nicole	161 ☐ Nicole
105 ☐ Blair	124 ☐ St. George	143 ☐ Allison	162 ☐ Horton

SILHOUETTE DESIRE, Department SD/6
1230 Avenue of the Americas
New York, NY 10020

Please send me the books I have checked above. I am enclosing $_____
(please add 75¢ to cover postage and handling. NYS and NYC residents please
add appropriate sales tax). Send check or money order—no cash or C.O.D.'s
please. Allow six weeks for delivery.

NAME_____

ADDRESS_____

CITY_____ STATE/ZIP_____